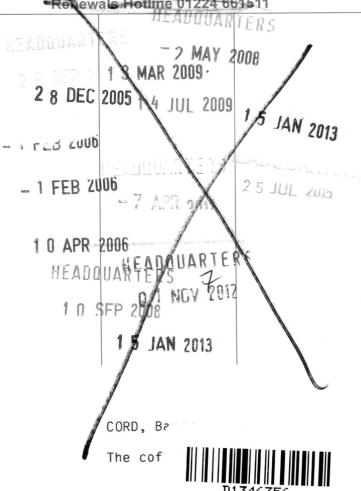

THE COFFIN FILLERS

The town of Apache Wells is primed for trouble. Sheriff Caulkins is nervous and there's no telling what might happen there any more.

Long Jim and Windy Harris come to Apache Wells, they're salesmen on the surface—but underneath there's a great deal more than meets the eye. Another salesman, Professor Eccleston, is in town with his caged tiger and is trying to sell his magic elixir Tigro.

There are dangerous characters in these parts and Zachary Stack the undertaker could have a lot of business coming his way...

6

THE COFFIN FILLERS

Barry Cord

GUNSMOKE

This hardback edition 2004
by BBC Audiobooks Ltd
by arrangement with
Golden West Literary Agency

ISBN 1 4056 8011 3

British Library Cataloguing in Publication Data available.

Printed and bound in Great Britain by
Antony Rowe Ltd., Chippenham, Wiltshire

I ABRIDGED ROBBERY

THE JOLTING wagon slowed at the fork in the rocky trail, and the driver turned to look suspiciously at the two wrangling pilgrims jogging slowly toward him along the other road. Behind them plodded a sad-faced burro, unmindful of the load on his back and the endless arguments of his masters.

"Yuh ain't got the sense of direction of a blankety-blank sheepherder," the pint-sized rider was telling his companion. "I tell yuh that's Goliath we're headed for!"

He straightened in his stirrups to squint down into the long dry valley where a town sprawled at the foot of a sheer-walled mesa.

"If I hadn't have let yuh talk me into taking this trail at that last fork—"

"We'd most likely still be wandering up there among those ridges," cut in Long Jim dryly.

Long Jim was six feet three and, despite a voracious appetite, was thin as a rail. He had a long, horsy face wrinkled deeply around humorous brown eyes and weathered by the passing of more than two scores in the saddle.

He was a few years Windy's junior and that fact was injected into every argument by the belligerent man who rode at his side. There was no subject Windy Harris wouldn't take up, and he argued with equal conviction when he was on sure ground, such as placer mining, cows and rustling, as when the subject was totally over his head.

5

Windy was a small man, crowding sixty, with a small, leathery face dominated by snapping blue eyes and a pugnacious button of a nose. His shapeless coat was too big over his narrow shoulders, and the Colt .45, jutting from the thonged down holster on his right hip, seemed too big for his hand. A white beard, speckled with brown, stubbled his cheeks and chin and an uncultivated moustache drooped around a tobacco stained mouth.

He and Long Jim had trailed together so long they had forgotten their first meeting and, despite their constant wrangling, more humorous than bitter, would have been lost without each other.

They were on their way to Goliath to look up Windy's nephew, but finding themselves near the town of Apache Wells they had decided to drop in on an old Virginia City friend, Hardpan Jeffries. For the past ten miles the trail had led through increasingly rocky terrain, and with every mile Windy had grown more certain they had taken the wrong turn.

He settled back in saddle now, Long Jim's remark feeding his belligerency. "Why, yuh long-laiged, dim-witted infant, if it wasn't for me—"

"Wait a minute!" Long Jim growled, waving a hand in the direction of the driver who was looking back at them. "Yonder's a gent who knows where he's headed. Let him settle the argymint. If it's 'Pache Wells, we turn into the nearest chow shack 'fore asking for Hardpan. If it ain't we'll belly up to the nearest bar an' drown our sorrows."

Windy snorted at the proposition. "Chow shack! We jest ate, yuh overgrown feedbag! Yuh an' that fuzzy-eared jackass, Blinky, cleaned out the last of the sow-belly an' beans less'n three hours ago!"

Long Jim ignored the observation. The wagon ahead of them was a long, boxlike vehicle with a light canvas top rolled up on three sides, revealing to Long

Jim's gaze a half dozen long pine boxes that looked very much like coffins.

"Howdy," Long Jim said, spurring up alongside the driver.

The man looked down, noting the thonged down holster on Long Jim's thigh and the Sharps buffalo gun that rubbed its stock against Jim's lean shank.

"Howdy yuhself," he nodded. He was a stringbean of a man, with sharp, stern features emphasized by bushy gray brows. A long black coat and a stovepipe hat gave him the look of a pious minister, but few ministers, thought Long Jim cynically, wore shoulder holsters.

"Yuh a native of that there town?" he asked.

The driver nodded. "Yep. Been living in Apache Wells nigh onto ten years. Name's Zachary Stack," he offered gravely.

Long Jim turned in saddle. "Yuh lose, Windy."

Windy bristled. "Yuh shore that ain't Blind Corners, mister?"

The driver frowned. "Plumb shore, hombre. Blind Corners is west of here, over yonder, behind them hills. I jest came from there." He turned and nodded toward the boxes in the wagon. "Bought these coffins in Blind Corners yestidday."

Windy scowled.

Long Jim's grin threatened his ears. "What's the best place in town for grub?" he asked. "Place where a couple of wandering pilgrims can get a man-sized meal?"

"Cassidy's," Stack said immediately. He glanced at the burro trailing them. Various kitchen utensils suspended from the pack.

He looked at Jim. "Salesmen?"

"Yep—salesmen," Windy said, speaking for Jim. He looked innocently at the driver, but Long Jim had to suppress a grin.

Salesmen they were—on the surface. But in that con-

7

glomerate pack under which the burro plodded they carried straight irons. Cheerful old reprobates, they roamed the wide domains, running off a few cows here and there, and generally winding up in some sort of trouble. More than one locality had misconstrued their appearance as a pair of saddle bums, to their later surprise and regret.

Windy said, "Yuh the undertaker?"

Zachary nodded. "Run the *Paradise Funeral Parlors*— only establishment of its kind in town," he added proudly.

Long Jim glanced at the coffins. "Anticipating a lot of business?"

Zachary shrugged. "Can't tell," he observed solemnly. "Apache Wells is primed for trouble. They's a heap of *dinero* locked up in the bank an' Bighead Nevens an' his outlaws are rumored to be hiding out in these hills. Sheriff Cal Caulkins is as nervous as an old maid with a man under her bed. . . ." He clucked at his team. "Nope—ain't no telling what'll happen in Apache Wells no more. Not with the Perfessor spouting talk about the power of the human eye an' making faces at that tiger he's got caged—"

"The Perfessor?"

"Yep. 'calls himself Perfessor Eccleston. Rolled into town about a week back. Claims he's the inventor of a tonic that'll make a rabbit step up an' kick his tiger in the teeth after a couple of snorts." Zachary shrugged. "Gents who've tried it says it tastes like pizen juice an' giant powder combined."

"Cripes!" marveled Windy, and Long Jim guffawed.

"Sounds like Apache Wells'll be mighty interesting," Long Jim opined. "Well—maybe we'll be seeing yuh there, Zach. Adios."

The trail into Apache Wells curled among tawny rocks

scattered haphazardly on the plateau, as if giants had sown them when the world was young. Where the trail dipped down toward town, Windy and Long Jim were halted by a stocky, black-whiskered hombre who stepped abruptly onto the trail from behind a rock.

"Howdy, strangers," he greeted. But he didn't look friendly. And the rifle in his hands was pointed their way.

"Going into town?"

Windy sighed and looked at Long Jim. Then he looked back to the guardian of the trail.

"Yuh objecting?"

"Maybe," the man replied. He looked them over casually, eyed the patient burro trailing Long Jim, and came to the conclusion they were harmless. Shifting his wad of tobacco into his left cheek he turned and nearly drowned a curious lizard that came out of a crevice to investigate.

"Guess you're all right," he said judiciously. "When yuh see the sheriff tell him I'm waiting for my relief, will yuh?"

"Sure," Long Jim agreed. They rode on. Evidently the sheriff of Apache Wells was taking no chances of a surprise raid by Nevens and his outlaw band.

There were few men in this section of the Southwest who had not heard of Bighead Nevens. A man with a huge, lion-maned head and enormous shoulders, it was said he could run down a wild horse and break its neck with his huge hands. Some of the tales told around chuckwagons and across bars rivaled those of the legendary Pecos Bill. However it may be, more than one lawman filled a shallow grave because of the outlaw boss.

No wonder the sheriff in Apache Wells was worried.

The trail veered away from a low, crumbly-faced

butte, and it was here that Long Jim and Windy discovered the uniqueness of the town ahead.

Just beyond the butte Long Lost Creek made a bend and doubled back on itself. Most of the year the creek was a dry bed of sand and stones—but repeated flood waters had ground out a narrow, deep canyon. Enclosed within this loop which formed an effective moat on three sides lay Apache Wells. Behind the town Copperhead Mesa rose in a sere, forbidding, unclimbable backdrop.

There was only one bridge into town, and it was up when they came to it. Some ingenious soul had engineered a crude cantilever affair, powered by a team of horses. The two wanderers could see the animals, standing patiently in the hot sun by the windlass. To their left a lean-to cast shade over an old character who sat with a corncob in his mouth and a shotgun across his knees.

"How do we get across?" Windy yelled.

The character stirred. A wrinkled face peered at them from under a floppy hat. He took the corncob from his mouth and spat into the dust. Then he shuffled to the patient horses. Grasping the nearest by the headstall he began to back them in a circle around the windlass.

The bridge came down slowly, creaking and groaning, and finally settled with a thud.

Long Jim and Windy rode across. The oldster held out his palm.

"That'll be two bits each, gents."

Windy frowned. "That's highway robbery—"

"Yuh mean bridge robbery!" Long Jim snapped. "We won't pay!"

The old character shifted his shotgun muzzle. "Two bits," he repeated firmly.

Long Jim and Windy paid him.

The bridge-tender tested the coins between tobacco-stained stubs of teeth. Nodding, he said, "Good luck to yuh," and went back to the waiting animals.

Long Jim and Windy swung away, hearing the bridge creak as the plodding team drew it up again.

II THE SUSPICIOUS LAWMAN

APACHE WELLS' first jerry-built structures began a hundred yards away from the bridge. Windy and Long Jim turned left into a wide, dusty street some wit had named Custer's Avenue, and paused to survey the structures sprawled on either side of them.

A score of warped frame buildings, most of them false fronted, baked in the late morning sun. At the far end Apache Wells petered out into boxlike, adobe huts, cracked and shaped into a composite of dust and filth and hung with crimson banners of chili.

Behind the false fronts they glimpsed broken corrals, littered lots with burros browsing on tin cans, a horde of terra-cotta children playing alongside pigs staked out to wallow in mire, and empty sheds sagging away from the prevailing wind.

Windy shook his head. "If Custer had seen this," he remarked, "he would never have made his last stand."

A coyotey dog with a floppy ear came out of an alley to greet them. Blinky, the burro, cocked a watchful eye at the yipping canine. Blinky was distrustful by nature and hated town dogs by instinct.

"Shore can't understand why Jeffries settled in this excuse for a town," added Windy. "Must have—"

"Let's find Cassidy's first," Long Jim interrupted hastily. "We'll ask about Hardpan after we eat."

They rode down Custer Avenue until Long Jim suddenly pointed to a one story shack wedged between

11

two false fronted structures with the imposing names of *Gertie Lou's Silver Palace* and *The Riviera.*

"There's Cassidy's," Long Jim said.

They drew up at the rail and dropped reins over the tiebar. Blinky brayed raucously and Long Jim turned and said, "Shut up, yuh long-eared jackass! We'll bring yuh some beans!"

They turned—and halted.

Windy's nose was two inches from a long-barreled Colt .45. His eyes traveled from the front sight along seven inches of blued barrel to a horny thumb clicking back a spike hammer. Then his gaze shifted to the slight man with the white goatee and the sheriff's star on his gravy-stained vest.

The lawman had a tic under his right eye.

"All right, hombres," he squeaked, winking rapidly. "Shed your hardware!"

Windy raised a hand in protest. "Yuh got us wrong, Sheriff. We're jest a couple of peaceable—"

"Whitey!" the sheriff snapped rudely, not waiting for Windy to finish. "Get up off your hind end an' relieve these galoots of their hardware!"

A long human with a young, slack-jawed face and a mop of white hair unfolded himself from a chair propped against *The Riviera*'s shaded front and slouched toward them. He shuffled like an old hound dog coming to its master after losing a rabbit.

"Kee-ripes!" he exclaimed, drawing Windy's Colt from the bantam's holster. "Little big for yuh, ain't it, grandpap?"

Windy bristled. "Listen, yuh spavined yearling! I was handling a shooting iron 'fore your ma made her mistake. . . ."

"*Shut up!*" the sheriff said.

Windy looked at the sixgun tickling his nose and shut up. Whitey relieved Long Jim of his weapon, chuck-

led at the weight of the heavy Frontier and turned
to the sheriff. "Want them put with the others, Cal?"

Sheriff Caulkins nodded. "Take their rifles, too," he
reminded.

Long Jim scowled. "You're making a mistake, Sheriff.
We ain't owlhooters."

The sheriff winked solemnly. "Can't afford to take
no chances—"

"Not with fifty thousand American pesos in that two-
by-four bank," grinned Whitey. Then he glanced at the
sheriff's scowling features and shrugged defensively.
"Aw—what the hell, Cal—they're only a pair of saddle
bums. Yuh can see that with half an eye—"

"That's all yuh ever see outa!" the sheriff snapped.
"An' yuh think like yuh had half a brain!"

Whitey grunted and dragged himself away toward
an adobe building across the street with iron-barred
windows and a sign that told newcomers here was:
Sheriff's Office, Apache County. Cal Caulkins, Sheriff.

"Lawd!" the sheriff moaned, raising his eyes heavenward. "The commissioners shore put one over on
us when they wished that long-laiged son of an ad-
dled jackrabbit on me for a deppity!"

"The good Lawd shore had something on his mind
when yuh was made sheriff!" Windy snapped. "What's
the idea of the hocus-pocus with our hardware? We're
free an' innocent citizens, seeking to earn an honest
living—"

"You're free, all right," the sheriff admitted, stepping back and holstering his Colt. "As long as yuh make
no wrong moves. As to being innocent"— He looked them
over carefully, his right eye winking disconcertingly—"I
reserve my judgment."

He waved a hand down the street to a squat stone
structure. "The town's yours—but keep away from the
bank. I'm plumb nervous about that there institution.

13

If you've come to stay in Apache Wells a while, you're welcome. If yuh wanna leave—come to my office. I'll see that yuh get your hardware back an' are personally escorted as far as the bridge."

He left them openmouthed and staring, until Blinky's raucous braying shattered the stillness, reminding them it was time to eat again.

III A GHOST FOR HARDPAN?

CASSIDY's was long and narrow with a lunch counter fronted by wobbly wooden stools. Cassidy was like his place, long and narrow. He was hunched over the cigar box that served as change box, chewing on an unlighted cheroot. He was younger than the two men who entered, but old enough to brood over a life he felt was misspent.

The counter man was a young, serious-faced fellow whose job was to take the food from the small kitchen opening where a Mexican cook alternately swore and sang over his pots and pans and hand it to customers.

Windy climbed onto a stool and looked up at the pencil-printed menu tacked on the wall behind the counter. Long Jim slid one leg across another, frowning at the lightness of his empty holster.

The youngster slid them each a glass of water. "What yuh having, gents?"

"Chicken," Windy said. "Ain't had a good drumstick to chew on since St. Looie."

The younger yelled the order to the cook and received a voluble answer generously sprinkled with Mexican cuss words.

"No chicken," he said, turning and picking up a pencil to draw a line through that item on the menu.

14

Windy scowled. Long Jim said, "I'll have the T-bone steak, lots of hashed brown potatoes an'—"

The youngster barked the order. Again the cook answered.

"No steak," the youngster interpreted, reaching up and drawing another line.

Windy and Long Jim looked at one another, then glanced at Cassidy. The lunchroom owner shrugged helplessly.

"All right," Windy snarled. "Make it two orders of pork chops an'—"

The swarthy-faced cook stuck his head through the opening and surveyed them with great deliberateness before answering the counter man.

"I know," Windy snapped as the youngster turned to him. "No chops!"

"What'n hell *have* yuh got?" rasped Long Jim testily.

The counter man shrugged. "Everything. But Sancho is temper'mental. He cooks what he wants. If he says no chops"—the youngster spread his hands—"there's no chops."

"Somebody's liable to sprinkle his temper'ment with lead," Windy growled. He turned to Cassidy.

"Yuh own this joint?"

Cassidy nodded.

"Why don't you fire him?"

Cassidy shrugged. "Ain't another cook inside of fifty miles—" He stopped as Sancho stuck his head through the opening and eyed him.

"Look," Cassidy said. "Why don't yuh go eat somewhere else?"

Windy started to bristle. Long Jim calmed him.

He looked at the counter man. "Ask him what's he's willing to cook."

The youngster turned to Sancho and got an immediate answer.

"Enchiladas," he said calmly. "An' frijoles."

"We'll take them!" Long Jim said before Windy could open his mouth.

Windy shrugged and glanced at Cassidy. "How's business?"

"Gone to hell," Cassidy answered morosely.

"No wonder," Long Jim said sympathetically. "With a cook like that—

"It's not Sancho," Cassidy explained. "It's that wandering medicine show gent. Used to be a time when the men an' women of Apache Wells could stow away victuals like any healthy citizen. This place used to be choked at every meal hour. Then this Perfessor showed up with his mangy tiger an' his Tigro tonic. Ain't a man had any appetite since they been guzzling that stuff."

Windy scratched his side whiskers in sympathy. The counter man came up with their orders and Sancho poked his head through the opening again. The sweat rolled down his coffee-with-cream face and formed little drops at the ends of his long black moustache. He showed white teeth in a grin.

"*Buenos fortunas, amigos.*"

Windy paused with a forkful of enchiladas poised in midair.

"What did he say?"

The counter man smiled. "I think it comes out 'Good luck, friends.' "

"Maybe we'll need it," Windy muttered. He took a bite, rolled it around in his mouth and started to swallow. His face stiffened. He gagged and grabbed for his coffee mug. The coffee was hot and burned his lips, but it was not as hot as the fire in his mouth.

Long Jim looked concernedly at him. Seeing the tears roll down Windy's cheeks he slapped him heart-

16

ily on the back. "What's the matter?" he asked solicitously. "Eat too fast?"

Windy regained his breath. He swiveled off his stool and started around the counter for the kitchen. "I'm gonna break every bone in that fire-setting son's—"

Long Jim clamped a big hand on Windy's shoulder and hauled the smaller man back. "Take it easy," he said mildly. "Ain't no sense running wild. This is the best enchiladas I ever ate."

The youngster leaned on his elbows and grinned at the spluttering oldster. "What's the matter, grand-pap? Can't yuh take a little pepper in your grub?"

"That ain't all I can't take!" Windy snapped. "Any more of your sass an' I'll come behind that counter an' stuff yuh through that hole into the kitchen!"

The counter man grinned. "All right, grandpap. I believe yuh."

He got up and walked to a customer who came inside and plunked himself down on a stool near the wall.

Windy rolled himself a smoke and watched Long Jim stow away both portions of the fiery food.

Cassidy said, "Strangers in town?"

Windy nodded. "Dropped by to look up a friend. Maybe yuh can tell us where Hardpan Jeffries hangs his hat?"

The question had a remarkably quieting effect on the others. Cassidy's jaw fell open and his cigar dangled from a pendulous lower lip. The counter man paused while yelling an order to Sancho, and the customer stiffened on his stool and stared at them.

Windy looked pugnacious. "What's wrong? You'd think I was asking about a ghost—"

The youngster recovered first. "You're right there, grandpap," he said quickly. "Jeffries *is* a ghost!"

Long Jim pushed his empty plate aside and scowled.

Windy's eyes went hard. "We've had a lot of hoorawing since hitting this town," he said quietly, and every man in that lunchroom felt the danger in this little man then. "From bridge robbers, winking sheriffs an' smart-alecky deppities down to temper'mental cooks. But when it comes to Hardpan Jeffries we quit playing!"

He leaned across the counter. "Now come again, button. An' hold a straight loop on your tongue. Where is Hardpan?"

The youngster's eyes grew serious. "Probably assaying rocks in hell," he replied coldly.

Cassidy cut in quickly. "Hardpan's shack is out of town about four miles north. Under the mesa. He used to come in here to eat, until he disappeared, close to a month ago."

"Disappeared?"

Cassidy nodded. "Last time he was in here Len here"—he jerked his head to the counter man—"staked him to a couple week's grub. Wasn't the first time Len staked him, either. Jeffries left promising to buy Len a string of lunchrooms, an' never showed up again."

Long Jim and Windy turned cold eyes on Len Stevens. The youngster's lips tightened. "Wait a minute, fellers! If you're getting ideas I might have killed Hardpan, forget it."

"Nobody knows for sure if Hardpan is dead," Cassidy put in quickly. "But some of the boys swear his ghost talks, if the moon is right—"

Windy plunked silver down on the counter and swung off his stool. "That's enough!" he snapped. "Come on, Jim—let's get out of this damn place."

Long Jim gulped down the last of his coffee and slid off his seat. He turned to look at Cassidy.

"Hardpan was a friend of ours," he said levelly, "an'

18

ghost or no ghost we're going calling. If something's happened to him we'll be back." He looked at the counter man. "To send him company in hell!"

IV PROFESSOR ECCLESTON

THE SHERIFF watched them ride out of town, heading for the mesa. He had just come out of the bank after reassuring himself things were as they should be in that institution, with Whitey following at his heels.

The deputy followed his gaze. "Funny pair of galoots, Cal. Wonder what they're up to."

"Keep an eye on them!" growled the sheriff, and headed for *The Riviera*. "Damn the whole cussed setup!" he mumbled. "Sam Bainter oughta have his head examined, depositing that much *dinero* in this bank. Bait for every owlhooter this side the Platte, that's what it is!"

He was still mumbling as he brushed aside the batwings of *The Riviera*, a squat, warped board structure whose front looked down on the squalor of Custer Avenue and a rear view that included a littered back lot, a stretch of desolate desert and distant, rocky hills.

Penn Trimble, the owner, had read a book once, mentioning the glories of the French Riviera and with the innocence of the thoroughly uninformed, pounced on the name for his establishment which in an earlier period had been simply, but more fittingly, named: *Trimble's Saloon.*

Sheriff Caulkins shuffled to the bar and hooked a heel over the rail. He held up two fingers, indicating his usual midafternoon snort. Trimble, a dirty white apron billowing over his enormous paunch, eyed him sleepily from the end of the bar. There were few customers in the saloon at this hour, for which Trimble heart-ily cursed the Perfessor and his cure-all libation: Tigro.

"Get it, yuhself, Sheriff."

He was hunched over the counter, his thick-jowled face resting in his hands. Cal went around the bar, found his brand of whiskey, and poured himself a drink. Then he found the credit pad under the counter, made his mark beside his name, and came back to the front of the bar. He drank his whiskey like a customer, foot on the rail.

Trimble roused himself. "When yuh gonna run that faker out of town, Sheriff?" he demanded for the sixtieth time, and for the same number of times the sheriff shrugged and answered, "This here is a free an' undivided country, Penn. The Perfessor has a legal right to set up business in Apache Wells, long as he minds his own doings, an' doesn't misinform the public—"

"What in hell yuh call that sulphur water he's peddling?" rumbled Trimble. "That stuff ain't fit for anything but to thin varnish—"

"Ain't had no complaints yet," Cal said, unmoved. "Some of the boys seem right perked up since they been taking Tigro." He scowled into his glass. " 'Sides, I got other things on my mind, Penn. I been losing hair ever since Sam Bainter sold his V-Bar-Two spread to that syndicate an' deposited the cash in our local institution—"

He turned and glanced at the man who entered. "Well, howdy, Perfessor," he welcomed. "We was talking about yuh. Lean an elbow on the bar an' have a snort."

Professor Eccleston, who signed his name with a half dozen alphabetical designations trailing, brightened at this unexpected welcome from the law. He was a tall, impressive figure in Prince Albert coat, slightly frayed at the cuffs, a black silk hat, white shirt, black string tie, melon kid gloves and malacca walking stick. He had a cast iron larynx, a cast iron stomach, and he held his liquor like a gentleman.

"Glad to drink with a representative of the law any time," he said, advancing to the bar. He had a sonorous voice.

Trimble scowled. The few loungers glanced up from their tables and fell asleep again.

Cal said, "Bring out that bottle, Penn—my special brand. Drinks are on me." And this time the mountainous saloon keeper obeyed, grumbling as he poured.

The Professor sipped the amber liquid. "The libation of kings," he said, rolling his tongue around in his mouth. "Almost as good as my special potion, Tigro. Now there's a drink for yuh, Sheriff. One bottle at my special closing offer of a dollar sixty-five an'—"

"Closing?" Trimble broke in, hopefully. "Yuh leaving Apache Wells?"

The Professor nodded. "In a couple of days or so. Can't play favorites, yuh know. Blind Corners is waiting impatiently for its share of my super tonic—"

"Glory be!" Trimble growled. He clamped a thick, sweaty hand around the whiskey bottle and poured. "On the house," he said generously.

Cal eyed him suspiciously, for Trimble had a reputation for being close-fisted. The Professor savored his drink, smacked his lips with pleasure, then flipped the rest of it down his throat with a flick of his wrist.

"Yuh are a gentleman an' a scholar, Mister Trimble," he praised, setting his glass down on the bar. "To show yuh my appreciation, I'm going to give yuh, absolutely free, a sample bottle of Tigro." He reached into a capacious pocket and hauled out a small, stoppered bottle of a vile green liquid that clouded as he shook it. "Should yuh want more I can be found at my rolling pharmaceutical establishment now parked in Baker's lot."

He paid for the next round, bought a bottle of Cal's brand of whiskey and turned away. Trimble watched him go, the bottle of Tigro still in his hand.

Pansy came down the bartop, stepping gingerly over the wet spots, her tail held high. She sniffed at the Professor's empty glass and ran a red tongue down into it. Her ears straightened and she made a plaintive, rumbling sound in her throat.

Trimble said, "Scat, yuh drunken feline!" and waved his thick arm at her. Pansy backed away, watching him, meowing like a bum begging for a drink.

"She ain't been the same since Gertie Lou's big tom got himself shot, yeowling on Cassidy's back fence," Trimble growled. "Now she's taking to drink—"

Cal pushed the boozy feline away from his glass. "Jest like a woman," he growled out of the deep conviction of bachelor experience.

The cat humped its back and spat at him, then turned and rubbed her ear against Trimble's hairy forearm. She sniffed expectantly at the bottle of Tigro.

Trimble's thick eyebrows made sudden V's as a thought parted his scalp. He ducked below the counter and found the small bowl in which he kept his change. He scooped out the coins, set the bowl on the counter, and poured the bottle of Tigro into it.

"Go ahead, Pansy," he said generously, thrusting the bowl under her nose. Cal hunched himself over the counter and watched.

The gray-striped cat eyed Trimble suspiciously. Then she dipped her head and sniffed. Her tail wagged sideways. She glanced up at the paunchy saloonkeeper with a trace of uneasiness in her eyes, then she decided to take a chance.

She took a half dozen quick laps at the liquid, paused, lapped again, then sat back on the counter as if a hand had come out of the bowl and pushed her in the face. She sat there, drops of the green liquid dripping from her whiskers, for about a second. Then she went straight up into the air with an ear-splitting yeowl and came down running, streaking across the saloon and vanishing under the batwings.

Trimble leaned back. "See what I mean, Cal?"

Cal drew the bowl to him and sniffed at its contents. Then he shook his head. "Maybe it ain't meant for felines," he observed, plucking at his goatee. "Leastwise, not for a lady like Pansy."

Professor Eccleston's covered show wagon was parked in the empty lot behind *Baker's Hay & Grain Store.* A weathered canvas awning shaded a box which the Professor mounted to deliver his "lectures." The tiger's cage, on wheels, was drawn up close to the awning, and supported one end of the cloth sign that told the citizens of Apache Wells to:

DRINK TIGRO: THE MAGIC ELIXIR Brought to you from the heart of darkest Africa. Trial size $2.00 Monthly supply $10.000

Windy pulled up before the wagon and peered in at the tiger asleep in a corner of its cage. The Professor was nowhere in sight, evidently preferring to deliver his sales talks in the cool of the evening.

Long Jim gravely surveyed the outfit. "Looks like the show we heard about in Tucson, Windy. If it is, things'll probably start popping around here."

Windy shrugged. "Not our truck. Anyway, we're plumb dehorned." He dropped his hand to his empty holster and scowled. "Damn that suspicious badge-toter."

They swung away from the medicine show wagon, following a road that led them toward the mesa. The road finally lost itself in brush along a dry watercourse, but now they could see the lone shack close under the cliff and they struck out for it.

The door was open when they got there, sagging on its one hinge. Sand drifted in over the framing. The board sides were gray and warped. A packrat ran out as they dismounted, ground-reining their animals. Blinky paused behind them and dozed.

The interior of the shack was crudely furnished. An empty box and some nail kegs had served Hardpan for table and chairs. There was a small wood-burning stove in a corner, its rusted stove pipe piercing the roof.

Long Jim walked to the oil lamp sitting on the box and touched the soot on the inside of the glass. There was dust everywhere in the cabin, but there were boot marks on the floor and crumbs by the box.

"Either Jeffries' ghost, or some other varmint, has been using this shack recently," said Long Jim, scowling.

They went outside and stood by their horses, undecided, trying to figure out what to do. They hadn't seen Hardpan in a long time, but if he had been killed they wanted to know who had done it.

It was quiet under the mesa. A rising breeze sprinkled sand through the open door as they stood there. Behind them the sun was starting down over the bend of the river. It cast their shadows against the cliff.

"Nothing we can do here," observed Windy, reaching inside his pocket for the remnants of his plug cut.

"Nothing we can do here?" floated down the echo from the mesa.

Windy stiffened. "Huh?"

"Huh?" said the echo.

Long Jim and Windy both looked at the sheer, tawny wall. There was nothing to see.

Windy gulped. "Hardpan!" he called.

"Hardpan!" came back the echo.

"Are yuh dead?"

"Dead . . . dead . . . dead . . ." answered the echo.

Windy backed toward his horse. Long Jim followed, his eyes searching the cliff.

"Is that yuh, Hardpan?"

This time the cliff remained silent. Long Jim tried again. There was no answering echo. The breeze picked up, scattering sand against the sagging shack.

Confused, angry, they rode back to Apache Wells.

V POLLY HANSEN

POLLY HANSEN crossed the street from her father's bank and strode into the sheriff's office. She was nineteen, lithe and strongly built, with reddish hair and sparkling blue eyes and no sense of feminine inferiority. She slammed the door open and crossed to Cal, who had been dozing behind his desk and stood with hands on her hips, eyes snapping.

"Where is he?"

Cal blinked rapidly. He was only half awake and he felt he was being invaded. He stuttered: "Wh- wh- where . . . is . . . wh- whoo?"

"My fiance!" Polly snapped.

He looked blankly at her for a moment and she rolled her eyes heavenward, slently asking spiritual help.

"Your nephew, Bill," she said, her voice flattening as she tried to control herself. "Don't yuh remember him?"

"Oh!" Cal slipped his boots from the scarred desk and tried to seek refuge in some old correspondence in a pigeonhole.

"Ain't yuh . . . seen him?"

"I wouldn't be here, yuh crop-eared mossback," Polly blazed, "if I had!"

Cal frowned. "Now that's no way for a young lady to talk to her prospective in-law, is it?" He ended on a plaintive note.

She sighed. "No, it isn't." Her tone softened. "I'm worried about Bill. I haven't seen him in two days."

He clucked at her. "Well, yuh know how young bucks are, Polly," he tried to soothe her. "Probably spending some time with the boys at the poolroom—"

She leaned over his desk, an incredulous look on her face. "*Mister* Caulkins"—she seldom addressed him this way unless she was utterly exasperated—"don't yuh remember?" As his face showed no recollection, she went on: "Yuh sent Bill out there"—she waved toward the outside—"to find out what happened to that old prospector, Jeffries!"

Cal scratching his head. "I thought he was back." He stood up, his jaw firming. "I'll send Whitey—"

"You'll send *who?*" Polly shook her forefinger under Cal's nose.

"I'll go myself," the sheriff said hastily. "Yuh go on back to the bank. I'll tell Bill you're looking for him."

She started to say something, realized the uselessness of it, and nodded weakly instead. She worked as a teller and her father was just as strict with her as he was with his other employees.

"I . . . I guess I'm just afraid for Bill," she said. "What with all that money in the bank, an' all the talk about outlaws—"

Sheriff Caulkins seemed to grow a foot as she weakened. He patted her shoulder.

"Just leave everything to me, Polly. I'll find Bill—give him a talking to."

He walked her to the door and stood there as she crossed the street.

Cal scratched his head, trying to remember what he had told his nephew. When his brother had died, Cal had raised Bill as his own son and he had a paternal interest in the young man.

"Damn it! I didn't send him anywhere!" he recalled. "He told me he was going up to the mesa an' have a look around . . . said he had a feeling things wasn't right. . . ."

He paused. Cal was not a complicated man and he could not handle more than one thing at a time. To hell with Hardpan Jeffries! He had the bank to worry about. How long would he remain sheriff if Bighead Nevens held it up? It made Cal nervous just thinking about it. He was getting on in years and jobs he could handle were scarce.

He walked down the street. The boy just wanted to get away for a while, he ruminated. Damn females are always pressing to get married. . . .

The local pool denizens shook their heads. No one had seen Bill in two days.

The sheruff walked into Cassidy's and slumped on a stool. He ordered coffee.

Cassidy was going over figures in his ledger. Cal said idly, "Where's Len?"

Cassidy shrugged. "Gave him the afternoon off. Kind of business I've been doing I might have to go to work myself. . . ."

Cal sipped at his coffee. "The Perfessor's leaving."

Cassidy brightened. "What do yuh want Len for?"

"He's a friend of my nephew . . . maybe he knows where Bill is."

"Bill disappeared, too?"

Cal bristled. "What do yuh mean—*too?*"

Cassidy said he was thinking of Jeffries.

The sheriff sighed. "Been people poking around, looking for gold in that area since I can remember. Ain't nobody found a dime's worth." He blew noisily into his cup to cool the coffee.

"My guess is the old coot jest drifted away." He looked at Cassidy. "Hardpan owed yuh for grubstakes, didn't he?"

"Not me," Cassidy replied. "Len. The boy has a sentimental streak, I reckon. . . ."

"Or a greedy one," Cal said morosely. He was not inclined this morning, to look kindly upon the young.

He sipped his coffee, then glanced up at the moustached cook who was singing a dirty Mexican ditty offkey. . . . Cal could see him through the kitchen opening.

"When yuh gonna get rid of that damn cook?" he growled.

"Shh. . . ." Cassidy lowered his voice. "Yuh want him to hear yuh?"

Cal sighed, got to his feet. "Guess I'll send Whitey to find Bill. . . ."

Cassidy, like Polly, raised his eyes heavenward. A perverse loyalty to Whitey caused Cal to say, "Damn it, he ain't as bad as all that!"

"No, he ain't," Cassidy agreed. "He's worse."

Cal tossed a nickel on the counter. Cassidy pushed it back to him. "Sheriffs have their privileges," he said. Then, sincerely, "It's a thankless job yuh have, Cal—and yuh ain't paid enough, far as I'm concerned."

The sheriff smiled and left the lunchroom in good mood for the first time in days.

VI WHITEY HOLLISTER

WHITEY HOLLISTER looked up from the box on which he sat, keeping vigil on the stone bank across the street. He gripped the .30-30 carbine across his knees and his eyes squinted purposefully as the sheriff came up.

"Nary a sign of them," he commented. "Been watching the front door an'—"

"What about the back?"

Whitey scratched his head. "Never thought of that." He shifted his rifle. "I'll go take a look—"

The sheriff cut him off. "I'll take over," he growled. "Yuh see Bill around anywhere?"

Whitey's brows puckered. "Thought yuh gave him a few days off—"

"Kee-rist!" Caulkins exploded. "A few days off! With Bighead Nevens an' his band of outlaws just waiting to rob the bank?" He shook his head, the tic jumping under his right eye.

"Aw—no need to get mad, Cal. I jest thought—"

"Quit thinking!" Caulkins snapped, "An' go find my nephew! Polly's worried, an' so am I. Damn fool hasn't been around in a couple days!"

Whitey stood up. "Bill missing?"

The sheriff stared at him. The apparent density of his deputy sometimes astounded even him.

"What in hell do yuh think I've been saying just now!"

Whitey shrugged. "Gee, Cal—yuh ain't feeling good, are yuh?"

The naïve concern in the younger man's tone disarmed Caulkins. He sighed, shook his head.

"I'll stand guard," he said. "Yuh look for Bill."

Whitey said promptly, "Sure, Cal." Then he frowned. "Where?"

Caulkins made a motion toward the mesa. "Probably went to check up on that fool prospector, Jeffries. . . ."

Whitey plucked at his chin as he followed the sheriff's gesture. "Say, them two ol' fellers rode out that way a while back," he recalled. His eyes narrowed. "Yuh think maybe they're up to something?"

"Maybe," the sheriff growled. "I ain't trusting anybody these days—not even yuh!"

Whitey looked hurt.

Cal took the rifle from him. "Take a look around Hardpan's shack. If yuh start now you'll get there before dark."

"What about the ghost?" Whitey's tone was nervous.

"Ghost!" Caulkins shook the muzzle of the rifle under his deputy's nose. "Ghosts can't pack a gun . . . all they can do is walk around, making moaning sounds"

Whitey's shoulders squared. "Hey, that's right, Cal." His tone hardned. "Ghosts ain't nothing to be afraid of."

"An' keep an eye on them two strangers," Caulkins said as Whitey started off.

Whitey nodded. "They won't even know I'm following them."

He strode off, a purposeful symbol of the law in Apache Wells. The sheriff shook his head as he took up the vigil on the box Whitey had vacated.

Whitey saddled his horse and rode out of town. Ahead of him the terrain looked deceptively level all the way to Copperhead Mesa, yet it was crisscrossed with ravines and sandy washes deep enough to hide a rider. Odd clumps of stone were scattered here and there, seemingly raked up out of the barren earth to provide a home for chuckwalla and leopard lizard.

Sagebrush made a silver gray carpet on the levels, manzanita made splashes of olive green along the gullies and ocotillo, past blooming, thrust their withered stocks like fragile spears into the hot sky.

Whitey kept to the maze of gullies. There was a wagon road, little more than ruts in the rocky soil, that went directly to Hardpan's cabin. But Whitey preferred to keep out of sight. He had been born on a hardscrabble ranch in the area and he knew this country like the back of his hand . . . he had hunted jacks and coyotes and deer in the wild country behind Copperhead Mesa and while he was only twenty-three years old he looked older. Whitey had heard there were towns and people and even oceans somewhere beyond, but Whitey confined himself to within fifty miles of Apache Wells. Blind Corners had been as far as he had ventured. He had found the town no different than Apache Wells and thereby concluded the world wasn't any different. He was a satisfied man. He had a job of some importance in his community, a roof over his head and he ate three meals a day. He couldn't understand anyone wanting more. . . .

He understood the sheriff's concern about the bank, but he did not share it. Whitey did what he was told to do, like an amiable dog wanting to please.

Now, an hour after entering the maze of erosion gullies behind Apache Wells he surfaced briefly, reining in under the protection of a dying oak, to study the terrain ahead. Hardpan's cabin was less than a mile away and closer he could see two riders heading back to town. He watched them closely, as the sheriff had said, until he was assured Long Jim and Windy were up to no tricks and were really headed back to town.

"Just a pair of saddle bums," he reaffirmed his earlier judgment. He shook his head in mild sympathy.

"Folks that old should be in a home where they can't get hurt. . . ."

He rode on now until he reached the cabin.

There was no one inside. Whitey looked around carefully, but he saw nothing that indicated anyone had been living here recently. He rustled a lint-specked piece of peppermint candy from his pocket and nibbled on it thoughtfully.

If Bill Caulkins had come here he had not stayed long. Whitey went outside and stood by his horse and stared up at the mesa wall behind the cabin. A steep slope of loose shale, scattered chunks of rock and parched earth from which, the Lord only knew how, desert shrubs sprouted and managed to survive, rose to meet the base of the cliffs which then towered an almost vertical two hundred feet above it.

There was no one here. Other than the two old codgers who had just left, Whitey reflected, there had been no one here in a long time. Hardpan was long gone. The stories about the old prospector's ghost were just stories, something to while the time away in the local saloons.

Whitey shook his head. Bill had probably sneaked off for a couple of days in Blind Corners. Not that he blamed him. Since word had come to Apache Wells that Big-head Nevens and his men were waiting to rob the bank Cal had been a hard man to get along with.

He took another nibble of his peppermint stick. There was nothing more he could do here, but he shrank from going back and telling the sheriff this.

"Bill!" He coughed a little self-consciously after the call, feeling like a fool.

The mesa flung the echo back at him.

He waited, not really expecting an answer. A small wind rustled through the brush beyond, accentuating the loneliness of the place.

"Damn it," he fretted aloud. "What would Bill be doing around here anyway?"

He turned to his horse, mounted.

A small rock slide came rattling down the side of the mesa. He jerked around, his hand dropping to his gun. His eyes squinted at the slope behind the cabin.

"Hey!" he called. "Anybody up there?"

The mesa flung his words back at him. Whitey's eyes narrowed. *Someone was up there, all right . . . watching him.*

He dismounted, ground-reining his animal. He called again, but nothing answered him.

Indignation spurred the lanky deputy. Goddamn it, maybe it was Bill up there . . . playing tricks. He wouldn't put it past Cal's nephew.

He started up the slope behind the cabin, his boots sliding on loose shale. Panting, he made his way to the base of the mesa wall.

A game trail, centuries old, wound along the base of the cliffs, making the footing here easier. He paused, getting his wind back. The sun was at his back, slanting across the base of the cliffs. It would be dark in another hour.

Uneasiness dampened his indignation. He drew his Colt, drawing some comfort from the feel of the heavy weapon in his hand.

"Bill! Is that yuh fooling around up there?"

Something moved above him. Earth and small rocks cascaded down and Whitey flattened himself against the mesa wall until the slide trickled off.

He yelled out angrily, but he was too close to the cliffs now and the mesa cast back no answering echo. He backed off a bit and looked up, but he could see nothing.

"Jeffries . . . ?"

A scream answered him, curdling his blood. It seemed

33

to come from further along the base of the mesa wall . . . from somewhere inside that rock mass!

Whitey stumbled back and slipped on the steep slope. He dropped his gun and clawed at the loose earth, finally halting his downward slide. On hands and knees, picking up his gun on the way, he crawled back to the base of the mesa wall.

Sweating, angry, Whitey looked up along the mesa wall. He waved his gun at it, threatening everything although he saw no one.

"All right," he said officiously, "whoever's up there, come on down!"

Nothing moved.

He started to pick his way along the base of the cliffs, following the game trail. Countless years had weathered deep fissures in the wall, some of the cracks extending into the rock mass as much as twenty feet. One of these lay just beyond a bulge in the mesa wall.

Whitey paused. He could make out boot marks, leading inside the crevasse. Something rustled inside. . . .

Whitey gripped his Colt firmly.

"Bill? That yuh in there . . . ?"

The cave swallowed his voice. Something moved inside again. . . .

It could be anything, he thought, *some small animal, maybe.* . . .

He took a step inside, his eyes adjusting to the shadows within. He saw nothing at first. Then, as he took another step, something started to float toward him, from the back of the shallow cave . . . a disembodied skull and two arms, dangling, jerking, moving toward him!

He backed off, firing wildly. The shots blasted his ears, magnified within that confined space. He forgot the steep slope just behind him. He backed off the

34

game trail and fell; twisting and scrambling he slid most of the way down the slope.

Bruised, battered and scared beyond measure Whitey picked himself up and ran to his horse. Mounting, he spun the surprised animal, sent it at a gallop back to Apache Wells. . . .

Two men watched Whitey's hurried departure from the cave entrance. One was Len Stevens, Cassidy's counter man. The other was an equally young man with an infectious grin, ruggedly handsome features and a shock of curly black hair. He needed a shave badly.

Len brushed at his cheek. "The damn fool near shot me!"

Bill Caulkins grinned. "Told yuh to stay closer to the wall, didn't I?" He let his gaze follow the distant figure of Whitey just before the deputy dipped out of sight. "Reckon it'll be a long time before Whitey comes out this way again. . . ."

Stevens was still a little shaken at his close call. "Yuh better get back to town, Bill. Your uncle must be getting worried to send Whitey out looking for yuh."

Bill shrugged. "Ain't Uncle Cal I'm worried about. It's Polly. She jest might decide to come up here herself—"

"Lawd forbid!" Stevens' tone was fervent.

Bill eyed him. "Hell, she ain't that bad!" His eyes crinkled with a sheepish grin. "Polly's jest a strong-minded gal—like her pa. . . ."

He took his badge from his pocket and pinned it on his shirt.

"Them two ol' fellers who rode up here before Whitey . . . yuh say they're friends of Jeffries?"

Stevens shrugged. "That's what they said."

Bill frowned. "They look pretty determined. They might come back"—he shot Stevens a quick look—"an' we

35

don't want them finding out what happened to Hardpan, do we?"

"Hell, let them look around," Stevens said. "They won't find anything. After a couple of days they'll ride away. . . ." He edged further out of the cave mouth and glanced toward the distant town.

"Be dark soon," he said. "Yuh better get back. I'll follow yuh a little later. Guess we'll have to lay low for a while—until things quiet down anyway." He chuckled. "I'd like to be back when Whitey tells his story. . . ."

He watched Bill make his way along the game trail and down into a brush-choked gully that led down to the level ground below. He and Bill never took the same way down, thus avoiding leaving too much of a trail.

Their horses were tied up in another gully a quarter of a mile away. Bill mounted his bay and rode back to town.

Stevens waited, hunkered on his heels, smoking a cigarette. He had a few things to do before he followed Bill. One was to get rid of the bones in the cave. . . .

VII "HE MISSING, TOO—?"

THE PROFESSOR was on his stand when Long Jim and Windy Harris arrived back in town; he was haranguing a growing crowd on the power of the human eye and the inestimable merits of Tigro.

Windy and Long Jim paused on the edge of the gathering to watch. The tiger was pacing inside his cage, a soundless, mindless shuffle that touched a chord of pity in the two men.

The Professor paused momentarily to eye the two

old men on horseback before continuing his long-rehearsed spiel.

". . . this magic elixir, brought to yuh at great personal expense an' danger from the heart of darkest Africa, home of the mysterious tattooed pygmies who, though small of stature, ladies and gentlemen, can quell the fiercest of jungle beasts simply by staring it down . . . their courage, of course, reinforced by the ancient an' mysterious ingredients embodied in this here tonic . . . the great, the one an' only Tigro. . . ."

Windy scowled as he turned to his companion. "They got tigers in Africa?"

His voice carried over the heads of the gathering to the Professor, who turned a cold eye in their direction.

"Do I hear a doubting voice, my friend—?"

Windy fixed him with a level stare. "Yeah," he drawled. "That big cat looks half starved to me. Why don't yuh feed *him* a little Tigro—?"

Long Jim intervened before the Professor found an answer to this blunt question.

"Come on, Windy," he growled. "We'll stick to the rotgut they serve in *The Riviera* . . . leastwise we'll know what *we're* drinking."

The Professor's hard voice followed them as they rode on. "Now there, ladies and gentlemen, are two men who could benefit greatly from my special formula, reverse the rigors an' frailties of old age, put the spring of youth back in their step. . . ."

Eccleston's voice faded behind them as they rounded the corner into Custer Avenue, passing Sheriff Caulkins sitting watchfully on a box across the street from the now closed bank. The sheriff eyed them with deep suspicion as they rode by.

They reined in at *The Riviera* and Blinky, turning to face Cassidy's, suddenly began to bray.

"All right, yuh long-eared foghorn!" Long Jim growled. "I'll get yuh some more beans."

Windy looked at him. "Yuh gonna eat again?"

"Might have a bite," Long Jim admitted. "An' Blinky's hungry. I'll meet yuh at the bar inside a half hour."

Windy snorted. "I don't know who's worse—yuh or that jackass!" he growled, turning to push through *The Riviera*'s slatted doors.

Long Jim went into Cassidy's. Sancho's temperament had changed. Long Jim could now have everything on the menu. He readily ordered steak and potatoes and a side dish of beans for Blinky.

Cassidy eyed him glumly from the end of the counter. "Did yuh talk to Jeffries' ghost?"

Jim nodded. "Talkingest spirit I ever jawed with. If that *was* Hardpan's ghost, he talks more now than he ever did when he was alive."

He looked around the empty lunchroom. "Where's that smart-alecky young counter man yuh got working for yuh?"

Cassidy shrugged. "Out somewhere." He scowled. "Might close up an' go home myself, if business doesn't pick up. . . ."

He took a cigar from a box at his elbow, slid it along the counter to Long Jim. Jim looked at him.

"On the house," Cassidy said. "Best customer I've had all week. . . ."

Long Jim settled back, lighted up.

"See anything at Hardpan's place?"

Long Jim shook his head. "Didn't look around much. Place looked like nobody'd been living there for a long time."

"That's what I keep telling the kid, Stevens. . . . Hardpan's long gone. But the kid keeps hoping. He laid out more'n a month's pay grubstaking Jeffries. . . ."

Long Jim scratched the gray stubble on his chin.

"Somebody's up on that mesa," he said, "somebody that sounded an awful lot like Hardpan. . . ."

"Trick echo," Cassidy came back promptly. "Something about that rock mass. There was a government geologist around here a while back. He explained it but most of it was way over my head. . . ."

"Way over mine, too," Long Jim said casually. "At least the voice was." He got up from the stool, laid money on the counter.

"Thanks for the cigar."

Cassidy acknowledged with a hand wave. "Come again." His voice was sincere.

Long Jim took Blinky's beans outside. He set the dish down before the burro and scratched his head.

"Something's crooked in this here setup, Blinky," he muttered. "That was Hardpan's voice me an' Windy heard, not an echo—"

He heard a voice down the street call for the sheriff and he looked up. He was behind Blinky and Windy's roan and not readily seen from across the street.

Zachary Stack, the undertaker they had met on the trail, was standing in the doorway of his establishment, waving to the sheriff. Sheriff Caulkins got up from his seat further down the street and headed toward the funeral parlors. . . .

Long Jim frowned. "Maybe the sheriff can tell us more of what happened to Hardpan than Cassidy or that closemouthed youngster he's got working for him let out. . . ."

He patted Blinky on the flank and started across the street.

Sheriff Caulkins was talking to Zachary Stack in the doorway of the *Paradise Funeral Parlors*. He was about to step inside with Stack when Long Jim hailed him.

Zachary looked annoyed. The sheriff waited, the tic jumping under his eye, as Long Jim strode up.

"How's the undertaking business?" Long Jim asked as he stopped beside the man in the stovepipe hat.

Zack shrugged.

Caulkins eyed Jim impatiently. "Yuh want something?"

"A few words," Long Jim said, nodding. "If yuh ain't too busy?"

Caulkins glanced at Zack, who shrugged. "Some other time, Cal," the undertaker said sourly and went inside.

"Yuh leaving?" There was a hopeful note in the sheriff's voice.

"Soon as me an' Windy find out what happened to our friend Hardpan," Long Jim replied.

"What happened to him?" Cal snapped back.

Long Jim scratched in his thinning hair. "I dunno. Thought yuh might have an idea. He wasn't at his place under the mesa—"

Caulkins sighed. "Mister, I got enough troubles without having to keep track of every fool prospector who goes digging around on Copperhead Mesa."

"We hear Jeffries' been missing for nigh onto a month," Long Jim interjected.

"Good," the sheriff growled irascibly. "Hope he never shows up." He started to walk back to his post up the street. Jim kept step with him.

"Feisty ol' boy, that friend of yours," Caulkins added. "Started more argymints in town than a barrelful of tomcats—"

"That he was," Long Jim agreed. "But Hardpan wasn't the sort to cut an' run. Could be something happened to him up on that mesa—"

Caulkins stopped by his box. "Look," he said earnestly, "I been losing sleep an' hair over the money in this bank. Tomorrow the bank examiner comes in. I got no time to worry about lost prospectors!"

He sat down, placed his rifle across his knees. "Go bother somebody else," he growled.

"Where's that dim-witted deppity of yours?" Long Jim snapped. He was irritated.

"Whitey? I sent him out there to find Bill."

"Who's Bill?"

"My nephew!" Cal answered. "Damn fool was a friend of Jeffries. Don't ask me why. That old codger could con the shirt off a dying man's back!"

Long Jim grinned, recalling this aspect of Hardpan. "Your nephew missing, too?"

Caulkins nodded. "He's due to get married in a couple weeks . . . at least that's what Polly says." He plucked at the goatee under his chin, eyed Long Jim with sudden suspicion. "Yuh shore you're friends of Hardpan's?"

"He never had better friends!" Long Jim snapped.

He started back across the street. The sheriff watched him, frowning. Then his attention swung back to the bank. Polly Hansen came out (she usually worked an hour after closing time, working on the books) and, spotting him, began to walk with determined stride toward the sheriff.

Caulkins steeled himself.

"Yuh find Bill?" Polly's voice was ominous.

"Well . . . he's around somewhere. . . ."

"*Did you find him?*"

"I sent Whitey. . . ." The sheriff cringed at the look in her eyes, then, remembering he was the law in Apache Wells, he said firmly, "We'll find him! Yuh go on home, Polly. I'll have Bill at your house tonight . . . for shore!"

"Where is he?"

Cal patted her shoulder. "Whitey's bringing him in," he lied.

"Bill isn't hurt?" Polly's lips trembled. "Is that why yuh—"

"No, no . . . nothing like that," Cal hastened to cut her off. "Bill was out there on the mesa, like yuh said, looking for that old prospector Jeffries. Guess he kinda forgot to come home, that's all."

Polly nodded. "I understand." Her smile was a bit tremulous. "Yuh know how my father feels about Bill? Feels he's got to prove himself—"

"Nothing wrong with Bill," Cal said staunchly. "Jest young, that's all."

He patted her shoulder again. "Yuh go on home an' pretty up. I'll have Bill there, don't yuh worry. . . ."

Mentally he crossed his fingers and prayed that for once Whitey wouldn't let him down.

Polly gave him a quick peck on the cheek. "Yuh know she said quickly, "you're really not as bad as most people say, Uncle Cal."

She left him to ponder this as she went quickly down the street toward the big frame house she called home.

VIII   OF MICE—AND MEN

LONG JIM was within spitting distance of *The Riviera* when he heard a voice call him. He turned and looked across the street to Zack, who beckoned urgently for Jim to join him.

Jim frowned, looked around. It was dusk, lamplight already shining in many windows. The street was all but deserted, most of Apache Wells' citizens either at home eating supper or in Baker's lot, gathered around Professor Eccleston's wagon.

He could see the sheriff talking to a young, pretty woman who seemed to be giving him hell. Long Jim shrugged and walked back across the street.

The undertaker said in a quick, *sotto voce* tone: "Yuh looking for Hardpan Jeffries?"

Long Jim eyed him without comment.

"I saw him," Zack offered solemnly.

Long Jim frowned. "Where?"

Zack cast a conspiratorial glance around the all but deserted street. "Come inside," he whispered. "I don't want it to get around."

Long Jim followed the horse-faced undertaker inside. The front room was furnished as a waiting room for the deceased's friends and relatives. There was an organ in a corner, a bad oil painting of black-garbed mourners around a coffin hanging on a wall, and incense smoldering in a tarnished brass Buddha on a table.

Heavy black drapes shut off a room beyond. Something made a sound in that room, something moved quickly, creaking across old floor boards.

Long Jim glanced in that direction, frowning.

Zack said heavily, "Damn the mice. . . ."

"Sounded like somebody whispering. . . ."

Zack smiled wryly. "Not in there." He raised his voice slightly. "Come on . . . take a look."

They walked into the back room where Zachary Stack did his embalming. There was a long wooden table in the middle of the room, worn smooth by repeated scrubbings. The odor of creosol and pine did not entirely obliterate the smell of formaldehyde. A window and a door looked out on an alley . . . the window had faded, sun-shredded curtains. The new pine coffins were ranged along the other walls, their lids closed. It was very quiet in the room.

Zack waved casually toward the coffins. "Jest looking ahead. If Bighead Nevens an' his bunch try to take the bank there's bound to be some killings. . . ."

"Good business sense," Long Jim nodded.

They went back into the waiting room. Long Jim rubbed his stubbled jaw.

"Yuh saw Hardpan?"

The undertaker nodded.

"Why all the mystery?"

Zack rubbed his hands together. "Hardpan did me a good turn once. I want to do one for him." He lowered his voice to a whisper. "Hardpan was in Blind Corners yestidday. I saw him."

"What was he doing there?"

Zack shrugged. "Jeffries cadged grubstakes an' drinking money from a lot of people in this town. Guess he figured they'd have his scalp if he showed up now. He was moving on, out of the country. He asked me not to tell anybody. . . ."

Zack paused, looked anxiously at Long Jim. " 'Course, yuh *are* a friend of his?"

Long Jim frowned. "Reckon Hardpan didn't find any gold up on that mesa . . . ?"

"Gold . . . up there?" The undertaker chuckled. "Hell . . . even the rocks aren't any good. Lots of folks poked around up there before Hardpan. All they ever found was an ol' Indian burial ground." He wagged his head wisely. "I figure Hardpan knew there wasn't anything up there . . . but the ol' codger had a way about him—"

"Yeah." Long Jim's voice was hard. He looked back toward the drape-shrouded embalming room. Something nagged at the back of his head.

He took a deep breath, dismissing the feeling.

"Yuh shore now, about seeing Hardpan in Blind Corners?"

Zack nodded emphatically. "Look—don't tell anybody in town. I promised Jeffries."

"I won't," Long Jim assured him.

The undertaker walked to the door with him. "Yuh an' your partner leaving town?"

Long Jim thought he detected the same note of hopefulness in his tone that had been in the sheriff's.

"In the morning," he said.

"Hardpan was headed west . . . said something about one of the gold camps around Denver. . . ." The undertaker glanced up the darkening street. "Might be hard to catch up with him. . . ."

"No hurry," Long Jim said. "Thanks for the information."

Long Jim crossed the street to *The Riviera*. Blinky brayed at him as he came by. The plate in front of the burro was licked clean.

Long Jim paused. He was vaguely irritated by Hardpan's disappearance. Maybe the old buzzard was in Blind Corners yesterday. But it was Hardpan's voice he and Windy had heard this afternoon, floating down from the mesa.

He pondered the problem. It was getting dark and Windy was waiting for him. Hell, let the little buzzard wait!

He picked up the plate and went into Cassidy's with it. There was a lone diner at the counter. The Mexican cook stuck his head into the kitchen opening and eyed him with lively suspicion.

Cassidy came out of a back room; he was suprised to see Jim.

"Brought your plate back," Jim said. He set it on the counter. "That young feller come back yet?"

"Stevens?" Cassidy shook his head. "Why?"

"Wanna ask him a few questions about Hardpan."

"You'll have trouble getting answers," Cassidy replied. "Len's pretty independent. . . ."

Long Jim's right hand slid instinctively down to his gunless holster; his eyes were cold.

"Seems like most folks in town are that way," he said.

Cassidy sighed. "Didn't mean to offend yuh, mister. But Len's young, an' he gets hardnosed about that ol' prospector. Folks have been ragging him about being taken in by Jeffries—"

Long Jim nodded. "Me an' Windy knowed Hardpan, off an' on, about twenty years. Most of what folks say about him is true. But he never ran out on any man who grubstaked him, unless he changed some since we saw him last."

He walked to the door, turned. . . .

"I'll be back later. I'm gonna ask the kid a few honest questions—an' I aim to get back some honest answers. Yuh tell him that, Cassidy!"

Blinky turned to look at him as he came out. "That's enough beans for yuh," Long Jim growled. He patted his horse's flank. Windy's roan nudged him, blowing noisily.

"You're right," Long Jim muttered. "Time to get yuh off the street an' into a nice clean stable—"

He paused, his attention suddenly caught by movement across the avenue. A figure had appeared in the alley between the funeral parlors and the building next to it. He jerked back quickly as he saw Long Jim. . . .

The long-shanked oldster frowned. It was just a glimpse, but the shadowy figure looked like Zachary Stack. What in hell was the town's undertaker doing, skulking around in his alley . . . ?

He glanced up the street, toward the bank. It was closed, windows darkened. The sheriff was no longer on guard across the street. The only sounds disturbing

46

the quiet came from Baker's lot, where the Professor appeared to be doing a brisk business.

Long Jim crossed the street to the *Paradise Funeral Parlors.* The alley was dark. He scratched his head. Something was going on that didn't feel right.

The undertaker's voice echoed in his head: "Damn the mice. . . ."

Hell, it was worth a look.

He eased into the alley, his big hand clamped around his gunless holster. It gave him a small sense of comfort. He paused by the window. A dim light flickered inside. He thought he heard voices. He tilted his head back for clearer vision and pressed his face against the glass.

That was the last thing he remembered . . . he sighed softly as the side of a hand-held Colt slammed across his head. . . .

IX WHITEY RESIGNS

WINDY FINISHED his third shot of Trimble's "special" and wiped his moustache with the back of his hand. He reached inside his shirt pocket for his tobacco sack as Trimble set them up again.

The day was gone.

Windy watched the big saloon owner light the overhead lamps. He scowled over his drink, wondering what was keeping Long Jim. The way his partner ate Jim could have gone through three meals by now.

Trimble came back around the bar. Windy was his only customer, but he was resigned to this sad fact of business as long as the Professor remained in town. Besides, he was a gregarious man, and Windy was company.

He reached for the bottle, but Windy held up a restraining hand. "Three's my limit." He glanced toward the door. "Got to check up on my partner . . . he was supposed to meet me here—"

"It's early yet," Trimble said. He was loath to see Windy leave. "Have one on the house." He poured out a refill before Windy could answer, pushed the glass toward the small man.

Windy hesitated.

"Sheriff been giving yuh a hard time?" Trimble's voice was sympathetic.

Windy shrugged, picked up his glass.

"Yuh believe in ghosts?" he asked Trimble.

"What kind of ghosts?"

"Talking ghosts."

Trimble leaned on his elbows and shook his head. "Nope. Ghosts are the spirit substance of dead men—an' dead men don't talk." He frowned at the small man. "Yuh been hearing stories about Hardpan Jeffries' ghost?"

Windy nodded. "Didn't believe it when I heard the story in Cassidy's. But me an' my partner rode out there an' heard it talk. It was Jeffries' voice all right." Windy spat out shreds of tobacco from his limp cigarette. "Said it was your likker that killed him."

Trimble looked indignant. "Goes to show yuh even ghosts have no gratitude today. Hardpan chiseled more free likker from me 'fore he disappeared than most men buy in a year—"

He broke off and turned toward the door as the sound of a hard-running horse clattering down the street seeped into the saloon.

"Somebody riding hell for leather," he grunted, and instinctively reached under his counter for his sawed-off shotgun.

Windy got his back against the bar and slid his hand down to his holster; he cursed softly, remembering where his gun was.

THE COFFIN FILLERS

The rider skidded to a stop just outside. There was only a bare moment before the animal quit running and boots pounded on the worn wooden step. Then the doors slapped open and Whitey burst inside.

The long-jawed deputy paused just long enough to glance around the saloon. He was white as a sheet. His face and hands were scratched, bruised . . . his clothes were torn.

He walked up to the bar, his eyes glazed, ignoring the shotgun in Trimble's hands. He shouldered Windy aside, picked up Windy's glass and downed it in one quick gulp.

Windy and the saloon keeper eyed him in shocked amazement.

Whitey banged the empty glass down in front of Trimble's nose. "Fill it!" he demanded. His voice was so strained it came out gargled.

Trimble eased his shotgun under the counter and obeyed as though hypnotized.

Whitey slammed the whiskey down again; he coughed, took a deep breath, glared at Trimble.

"I'm quitting!" he snarled. "An' don't yuh try to talk me out of it, neither!"

Trimble shook his head in utter disbelief.

"Yuh hold him," he whispered to Windy in a tone loud enough to reach across the room, "while I go fetch the sheriff."

Whitey backed off, dropped his hand to his gun. "Nobody's gonna hold me!" he announced grimly. "An' to hell with the sheriff. Yuh can tell him I said so—"

"Tell me what?" the sheriff asked harshly. He was coming in behind Whitey, his tic jumping under his eye.

"Damn fool!" he continued, glancing at Trimble. "Riding past the bank like that! Near shot him 'fore I saw who it was!"

49

Whitey reached for the bottle and poured himself another drink which he gulped down immediately.

Trimble clamped his big palm over the bottle. "Who's paying for this?" he demanded. "Yuh—or the county?"

"Ask the sheriff!" Whitey snarled.

He turned, glared at Windy. "Yuh say you're a friend of Jeffries?"

Windy raised a hand in a gesture of peace. "Look, deppity, I'm just a peaceful bystander here. . . ."

Whitey swung around to the sheriff. "To hell with your nephew!" he snapped. "I'm turning in my badge—" His fingers began to fumble with the star on his shirt.

Cal Caulkins looked alarmed. "Yuh can't do that!" he protested. "Not now. Not with all that money still in the bank—"

"Hell I can't!" Whitey turned, reached for the bottle, but Trimble jerked it back.

The sheriff put a hand on Trimble's huge forearm. "Let him have the bottle," he said. "The county will stand the expense."

Trimble looked doubtful, but he released his hold on the bottle. Whitey promptly poured himself another drink and downed it.

Windy eyed him, marveling. "Does he do this all the time?" he asked the saloon keeper.

"Never saw him take a drink before," Trimble growled.

Caulkins pulled Whitey away from the bar. "Did yuh find Bill?"

"Hell with Bill!" Whitey snarled.

Caulkins' goatee jerked like a billy goat's. "Yuh look like yuh fell into a meat grinder. What happened—?"

"Hardpan's ghost, that's what happened!" Whitey thrust his jaw toward the sheriff. "Heard him scream up there, under the mesa . . . then I saw it!" He turned and filled another glass of the raw whiskey, gulped it down.

Trimble stared in openmouthed wonder. "One hundred proof raw whiskey." He looked at Windy. "Never saw a man who could stand up to it the way he does."

The sheriff was getting mad. "Saw what, yuh fool?" He grabbed Whitey, pulled him away from the bar again.

"Hardpan Jeffries!" the white-haired deputy mumbled. "Or what was left of him. . . ."

Windy stiffened. "Yuh found Hardpan's body?"

Whitey nodded. "Skull an' two arms . . . all that was left . . . waving . . . coming at me. . . ."

He stiffened, a strange look coming over his face. His eyes crossed. "Need 'nother drink. . . ." He started to turn. A strange gargling sound issued from his lips. Then he collapsed like a rapidly emptying sack of grain. He fell against the bar and slid down, curling in a limp heap over the brass rail.

Trimble leaned across the counter and craned his neck for a look at the deputy. He shook his head. "Was wondering how long it'd take 'fore it hit him."

The sheriff eyed his inert deputy with disgust. "Gone loco," he muttered. "Goddamn it, I've had enough of Jeffries' ghost. If I didn't have to stay here, minding the bank, I'd ride out there an'—"

Windy cut in, his voice cold: "I don't know what he saw out there, Sheriff, but I'm sure as hell gonna find out. Soon as I find my partner."

The sheriff eyed him with sudden suspicion. "Ain't he here with yuh?"

Windy waved to the otherwise empty saloon. "Not unless he's turned into a ghost too."

The sheriff scratched his head. "I talked to that long drink of water less'n a half hour ago."

Windy took a hitch at his empty holster, scowled. "Long Jim better be around," he said ominously. "Or somebody's gonna have to come up with an answer, quicklike."

The sheriff started to stop him as Windy started out, but thought better of it as he saw the look in the older man's eyes. He turned to Trimble.

"What're we gonna do with him?" he growled, indicating Whitey.

Trimble came around his bar and looked down at the deputy. He shook his head. "Not much we can do." He shrugged. "Give me a hand with him, Sheriff. We'll let him sleep it off in my back room. . . ."

X "AIN'T NO FOOL LIKE A YOUNG 'UN!"

WINDY HARRIS paused on the walk outside *The Riviera* and eyed the town with a jaundiced eye. It was a warm night, quiet and deceptively innocent of trouble. But something had happened to Long Jim. Windy felt it in his bones, like the approach of winter. . . .

He crossed the street to the lunchroom and Blinky brayed an impatient welcome as he approached. The two saddle horses eyed him with reproachful regard.

Windy paused at the hitchrack and patted the flanks of the horses. Scowling, he stepped into Cassidy's.

Cassidy was chewing on a cigar as he revised his menu. He didn't look up as Windy came in, but the cook stuck his head through the opening and said something under his breath.

Windy ignored him and stopped by Cassidy.

"Seen my long-laiged partner around?"

"Was in here," Cassidy replied, drawing a line through an item. "Left about ten minutes ago."

Windy glanced at the cook, who retreated, scowling, into his territorial domain, the kitchen.

"Where's that young helper of yours?"

"Len?" Cassidy looked up now, glanced at his watch. "He's due in now. He has to help Sancho with the supper rush—"

"What rush?"

Cassidy sighed. "Yeah. Well, anyway, he should have been back ten minutes ago. That's the trouble these days," he grumbler, "can't trust the help anymore. Now when I was a youngster—"

Windy retreated before Cassidy got started on his pet peeve.

He stopped by the burro and studied the town. The sheriff came out of *The Riviera*, eyed him briefly, and walked toward the bank.

Where in the devil was Long Jim? Windy scowled. It wasn't like Jim to go off and leave Blinky. For that matter where was Len Stevens?

He glanced up and down the street. It was deserted. The bank was locked up, its windows dark. Windy wondered if the sheriff had gone home, or was he lurking around somewhere, jumpy as a dog with a skinful of fleas. He swore under his breath. He could feel trouble in the still air. The lightness at his right hip annoyed him.

Law or no law, he decided, *I'm going to get my shooting iron. Don't feel right without it!*

He went up the street, turning the corner toward the squat adobe building with the barred windows. A sign over the door said it was the sheriff's office. He tried the door but it was locked.

Windy backed off a bit, studied the barred window. A voice behind him asked, friendly like: "Yuh looking for something, grandpap?"

Windy turned. A man stepped down from a horse and came toward him. He wore a badge on his shirt. He was young, but he hadn't shaved in several days. He had a likable grin on his face.

But he kept his hand on his holstered gun as he walked toward Windy. The oldster waited until he was close.

"Who're yuh?"

"Bill Caulkins," the man replied.

Windy eyed him suspiciously. "I didn't see yuh ride into town."

Bill's grin widened. "Your eyesight's failing, grandpap. I rode right by yuh, followed yuh here. . . ."

"Like hell yuh did!" Windy glanced toward the alley out of which Bill had come. "If you're Bill Caulkins your uncle's looking for yuh. . . ."

Bill sighed. "Uncle Cal's always looking for somebody." He gestured toward the door. "Yuh want something in there?"

"My gun!" Windy snapped. "I'm planning to leave this cussed town!"

Bill chuckled. "I see Uncle Cal's still dehorning all strangers. . . ."

He walked to the door, unlocked it with a key on his key chain.

"Your partner leaving with yuh?" he asked.

Windy paused just behind him, his eyes narrowing. Bill turned, his face sobering. "Yuh have a partner, don't yuh? All yuh ol' fellers do."

Windy nodded slightly. "Yeah."

Bill pushed the office door open. "Okay, pop."

Windy followed him inside.

Bill waved to several guns piled on the floor beside the locked gun cabinet. "Which one's yours?"

Windy picked up his Colt, checked it, slid it into his holster. The weight at his hip eased the frustration inside him.

"I'll take my rifle, too," he said.

Bill walked to several rifles propped up against the

gun cabinet, picked up the Sharps whose muzzle towered above the others.

"Cripes," he marveled. "Ain't seen a cannon like this since—"

Windy put a hand on his shoulder, jerked the young deputy around. "Yuh haven't seen anything yet!" he snapped, hooking the muzzle of his Colt into Bill's lean stomach.

He reached around and pulled the astonished lawman's gun from his holster and tossed it behind the desk. Then he stepped back, made a motion with his gun muzzle.

"Get inside one of those cells, deppity—"

Bill's mouth snapped shut, an angry light in his eyes. "Listen, yuh ol' fool!" he said grimly. "Put that gun away 'fore I—"

He made a sudden lunge for the old man. Windy chopped down with his Colt and Bill fell. Windy stood over the unconscious youngster, shaking his head.

"Ain't no fool like a young 'un!"

He found rope on a dusty cabinet and he used it to tie Bill Caulkins. Gagging him with his own neckerchief, Windy dragged the young deputy into one of the two cells, the door of which was open. The other was unoccupied. He rolled Bill onto a bunk, leaving him on his back. He went out, closing and locking the cell door with the key still sticking in it.

He stopped to pick up Long Jim's Colt, which he thrust inside his belt where it was hidden by his shapeless coat. He decided against taking the rifles.

The weight of his .45 felt good against his thigh. He went out, closing the door behind him. Assuming an innocent air, he sauntered back to Custer Avenue.

XI GERTIE LOU

GERTIE LOU came out of her office and glumly surveyed the empty interior of *The Silver Palace*. Business had fallen to almost zero since Professor Eccleston's advent to Apache Wells.

Gertie felt indignation mount within her ample bosom. If that shyster remained in town another week, every honest establishment in Apache Wells would go broke.

She made her way to the bar where a meek, lantern-jawed man was polishing the cherrywood bar by the window and staring dreamily into the street.

"Jerry!"

The bartender jumped and automatically began to polish faster. Then he sidled over to where she waited impatiently.

"Make me one of them cherry specials!" she snapped. "And don't forget to put in the lemon like that whiskey drummer showed yuh."

Jerry nodded. Things were going to the dogs in Apache Wells, he reflected sadly. Used to be a time when Gertie drank her whiskey straight, like any decent person. . . .

He dropped the cherry into the concoction and set it on the bar in front of her.

"Been feeling a mite poorly, Gertie," he said absently. "Maybe a shot of that tonic, Tigro, might help perk me up a bit—"

"*Tigro!*" Gertie's voice blasted his eardrums. "If yuh mention that in here once more I'll stuff yuh into one of the empty beer kegs." She shook an admonishing finger at the cringing bartender. "What yuh need is to quit sneaking drinks behind my back! Next time I catch yuh guzzling out of my private bottle I'll perk yuh up without benefit of that sulphurwater the Perfessor calls Tigro!"

She had another drink, then wandered back into her office. She stared moodily at the picture of a stern-faced, thick-moustached man hanging on the wall behind her desk.

"Things ain't been the same, Harry," she said disconsolately, "since yuh left me. People are always trying to take advantage of frail widows like me."

Gertie was five feet eleven in her socks and weighed one hundred and ninety pounds. She was her own bouncer, the duties of which she discharged promptly and effectively. But it pleased her to take on a humble dependence in her soliloquies with the picture of her departed husband.

She pulled open her desk drawer and took out a bottle of rye. In the privacy of her office habit reasserted itself. She sighed heavily and tipped the bottle to her lips.

The batwings creaked as she was slipping the bottle back into the drawer. The sound picked up her spirits. *A customer?*

She waited, checking her appearance in the mirror by the door. Gertie Lou was slightly past her prime, but she still considered herself in the marriage market.

Then she heard Jerry squeal and the coyness left her face as she grabbed the shotgun she kept in her office for emergencie and yanked open her door.

A pint-sized figure in white whiskers was holding Jerry across the bar, one hand tangled in the bartender's black string tie, the other holding a long-barreled Colt under his nose. . . .

Gertie Lou lifted her voice in an unladylike roar: "Hey, yuh!"

Windy turned. He saw the woman advancing on him with the shotgun and he stepped back, loosening his hold on Jerry's tie. The bartender staggered back against the wall shelves and gingerly felt his throat.

"Holdup, eh?" Gertie shoved the muzzle under Windy's nose. "Why yuh pint-sized, spavined ol' fossil, I'll blow a hole in yuh big enough to—"

Windy put his left hand under the muzzle and lifted it toward the ceiling. "Easy, ma'am," he said quickly. "I wasn't trying to hold anybody up." He turned to Jerry as Gertie brought the muzzle back down and jammed it against his stomach. "Tell this goddamn Amazon what yuh said!"

Gertie looked from Windy to her bartender. Jerry gulped. "It was nothing, Gertie—"

"Nothing?" Windy snarled.

The bartender shrank back against the shelves, looked to Gertie for help.

"He walked in here an' asked if I had seen his partner around." Jerry felt of his aching throat. "All I said was 'Yuh mean there's another one of yuh in town . . . ?'"

He cringed as Windy eyed him. "Hell, I didn't mean anything, mister." His voice grew sullen. "It's been one of them days. I was just trying to liven things up a bit—"

Gertie scowled as she pulled the muzzle away from Windy's middle.

"A mite testy, ain't yuh, pop?"

"A mite," Windy admitted coldly. "Who're yuh?"

"I'm the owner of this establishment," Gertie replied She backed off and looked him over critically. He was not what she had in mind, matrimonially speaking, but then, few prospects ever came to Apache Wells.

"I'm just a poor widow," she went on, "defenseless an' alone, trying to run an honest saloon. . . ."

Windy spotted the look in her eyes and shied off.

"Sorry I got ruffled," he told the bartender. "But me an' Long Jim, my partner, have been hoorawed since we got here. A doggone suspicious sheriff, a sassy white-haired deppity, a crazy Mexican cook—"

"Give the gentleman a drink," Gertie cut in, fixing her bartender with a cold stare. "On me," she said generously to Windy, setting her shotgun down on the counter. "Might as well give it away . . . you're the first customer that walked in here today."

Windy took the drink, tasted it. "Same brand they serve in *The Riviera*—"

Gertie took the drink away from him. Her eyes snapped fire. "Yuh a friend of that pirate, Trimble?"

"Never saw him 'fore today," Windy answered.

She kept her grip on the glass. "What yuh doing in town?" Her gaze narrowed. "Yuh ain't one of them outlaws Cal's so jumpy about?"

"No."

"Yuh aiming to rob the bank?"

He looked at her, frowning. "Ma'am," he said sincerely, "it never entered my mind."

She looked disappointed. "Wouldn't bother me," she told him. "I keep my money in a sock. Always figured ol' Sam Bainter was a fool." She finished Windy's drink, made a face. "Imagine, putting good money in somebody else's bank. . . ."

She beckoned to Jerry, who hastily refilled the glass which she then slid to Windy.

"Go ahead, drink up."

Windy picked up the whiskey glass.

She pressed up closer. "Yuh ain't by any chance a friend of that slick medicine man who calls himself Perfessor Eccleston?"

Windy tossed the drink down before answering.

"Only friend me an' Long Jim have in town is Hardpan Jeffries. We stopped by to visit with him for a spell an'—"

He paused as Gertie Lou snatched up the shotgun, clicked back on the hammer.

"Jeffries, eh?" She motioned with the yawning, deadly muzzle. "Pay up, mister. Four bits!"

Windy scowled. "I thought yuh said the drink was on the house?"

"I changed my mind. Any friend of Hardpan's ain't no friend of mine!"

Windy dug in his pocket and brought up a half dollar which he tossed on the bar.

"Maybe that's the trouble," he said coldly. "Everybody in town is too busy with their own problems, like hating the Perfessor or watching the bank, to worry about what happened to an ol' prospector named Jeffries."

He walked slowly to the door, paused, looked back. "An about your whiskey, ma'am," he said calmly, "I find the likker they serve in *The Riviera* a mite better—"

He ducked out before Gertie could get her shotgun muzzle around. . . .

XII WHO'S BEEN SNOOPING?

WINDY PAUSED on the walk in front of the saloon and eyed the horses still tied up in front of Cassidy's lunchroom.

Blinky turned and brayed his grievance, the sound carrying up and down Custer Avenue with jarring discord.

Windy scratched his head. He was more worried than he cared to admit. It wasn't like Long Jim to forget the jackass . . . they had things in common . . . like eating. Blinky would eat anything Long Jim set in front of him, but he preferred fiery Mexican beans above all else. And Long Jim seldom went more than a couple of hours without eating something, even if it was only chewing on a piece of hardtack or dried beef.

He looked toward the bank, but it sat there, solid and impregnable. A man sat on the box set up across the street . . . a solid-bodied, black-whiskered man with a rifle across his knees.

Probably relieving the sheriff, Windy speculated. Whole town's crazy.

Down the street he could hear the murmur of Professor Eccleston's voice as he made his spiel, although he could neither see the man nor the wagon. He thought of the old tiger lying asleep in the cage and he felt a flash of sympathy for the animal.

He was about to cross the street and go into Cassidy's again, when:

"*Psssst!*"

Windy eyed the tall, gaunt man in the doorway of the *Paradie Funeral Parlors.*

Zack Stack made a quick "come on" motion with his hands. He looked nervously up and down the street, as though afraid of being seen.

Windy dropped his hand down across his gunbutt and sauntered over.

"What's your trouble?" he demanded. "Not enough business?"

The undertaker cracked a sour smile. "Yuh looking for your partner?"

Windy said he was.

Zack stepped back inside the funeral home. "Come on," he whispered.

Warning raised a suspicious itch in Windy. He stepped inside, wary and alert. The undertaker was already

61

across the reception room, parting the heavy drapes of a doorway at the far end.

"Been all kinds of strange goings-on in town," the undertaker was saying. He turned and looked at the old man. "Your partner—he's in here."

Windy paused, settling his weight on his toes . . . his hand gripped his gunbutt.

"What's in there?"

Zack waved impatiently. "Come on."

Windy crossed the room to Zack's side and looked past him, into the room beyond. A lamp, turned down, cast just enough light to show him Long Jim lying on the plank table where Zack did his embalming.

Windy's hand came up with his Colt. He hooked the front sight under the fourth button in Zack's white shirt.

"Hell, he ain't dead," Stack said hastily. "I found him a few minutes ago, lying out there, in the alley." He gestured toward the back door. "He was groaning a little, so I knew he wasn't dead. I hauled him in here." Then, reacting to Windy's look, "I couldn't let him lie on the floor, could I?"

Windy walked to the side of his partner, who was beginning to stir. A small groan came from between Long Jim's lips. He looked up at Windy, his eyes out of focus.

"Scared the hell outa me," Windy said. Then, angrily: "What in hell were yuh doing out in the alley?"

Long Jim squinted up at his partner. His head ached with dull throbbing pain. There was a bad taste in his mouth. He rolled his head to look at the undertaker standing by Windy's side.

"What'd yuh give me . . . ?"

"Goat's milk," Zack said. "Spiked with ground *peyote*. Ol' Indian remedy . . . good for headaches. . . ."

"Aaagh!" Long Jim swung his legs over the side of

the table and sat up. His vision was still blurred. His stomach was queasy.

"Chasing pink cows . . ." he mumbled. "All of them mavericks . . . chased them over purple cliffs . . . all kinds of lights in the sky. . . ." He paused, looked at Windy. "Where've yuh been?"

Windy looked disgusted. "Waiting for yuh in *The Riviera.*"

Long Jim looked around the dimly lighted room. The coffins were in shadow, ranged along the walls of the room. He recoiled slightly, squinted at Windy.

"What happened?"

Windy glanced at Stack. The undertaker shrugged. "Like I told yuh, he was lying out there, in the alley. I thought he was drunk—"

"Someone slugged me," Long Jim said. His fingers went up to probe at the goose egg above his right ear.

"What in hell were yuh doing snooping around in the alley?" Windy snapped.

Indignation now invaded Zachary Stack's voice. "Yeah," he growled. "What in the devil were yuh doing out there?"

Long Jim put his aching head between his palms for a moment. "Cripes, I don't know," he snarled. "Don't even remember being there. . . ."

He stood up, took a deep breath, then decided he'd live. But the grin on his face was sickly.

Windy inquired solicitously: "How's your head?"

"Big as a balloon," Long Jim growled. "It ain't my head so much . . . it's my stomach. . . ."

"Yuh hungry again?"

Long Jim considered this with grave concentration. "Yeah—maybe that's it." He eyed the gun on Windy's thigh. "Hey . . . the sheriff get generous all of a sudden?"

Windy took Long Jim's Colt from under his coat, handed it to his partner.

"Town's got more danged deppities running around loose," he said cryptically. He glanced at Zack. "Thanks for calling me in."

Stack spread his hands in a gesture meaning it was nothing. "My pleasure. Never did like Cal."

He turned to Long Jim. "Yuh still going to Blind Corners?"

Long Jim frowned. "What's there?"

Zack sighed. He walked to the door with them, looked out.

"Ain't no sign of them outlaws. I think the whole thing was cooked up by the sheriff to make himself important . . . get a little extra overtime, too. . . ."

Windy eyed his partner. "Yuh tell him yuh were going to Blind Corners?"

Long Jim scratched his head, winced at his fingers touched the swelling. "Seems like . . . yeah. . . ." He turned to the undertaker. "Something about seeing Hardpan, wasn't it?"

Zack nodded. "Saw him in Blind Corners yestidday." He shook his head. "Can't say I blame Jeffries. Half this town was after his skin. . . ."

Long Jim nodded. "Yeah . . . I remember . . . some of it, anyway" He glanced back inside the room. "Remember being in here earlier an' yuh telling me that. . . ."

He put a hand on Windy's shoulder. "I've had enough of this town. Let's get out of here."

The undertaker looked pleased.

They thanked him and went outside, crossing the street again, to stop by their mounts. Blinky tried to bite Windy. The burro was in bad mood.

Long Jim walked to his horse's side, started to

64

mount. He paused, turned to Windy. "Where's my rifle?"

"Back in the sheriff's office."

Long Jim stepped back. "I ain't leaving without that Sharps. . . ."

"We ain't leaving," Windy said. "Not just yet, anyway."

"What do yuh mean, not just yet? If that horse-faced embalmer was right about seeing Jeffries in Blind Corners, we're wasting time—"

Windy plucked at his chin whiskers. "Maybe," he said calmly. "But I figure we oughta ride back to Hardpan's cabin an' look around that mesa a bit—"

"Why?"

"The sheriff's deppity, the one they call Whitey, saw something up there this afternoon. He rode back into town a few minutes ago while yuh was lying in there, chasing pink cows, an' drank himself blind in *The Riviera.*" Windy frowned. "He kept talking about seeing Hardpan's skull coming at him. Anyway, I reckon we better ride on out there an' take a good look around. . . ."

"Not on an empty stomach," Long Jim growled.

"We ain't got time!" Windy snapped. "Sheriff spots us wearing guns an' he'll slap us in jail. . . ."

"What about them?" Long Jim demanded, pointing to the horses. "They been tied up here all day. . . ."

"We'll stop by the stable, water them, pick up some feed. . . ."

They mounted. Long Jim turned a longing look toward Cassidy's.

"Come on," Windy growled. "Do yuh good to go hungry once in a while. . . ."

They rode off, looking for the stables.

XIII "KEEP AN EYE ON THEM, CAL"

SHERIFF CAULKINS lived in a boarding house a block south of the bank. Supper went with the room, but he usually passed this up, preferring to eat at Cassidy's. Ma Johnson, the boarding house owner, presided over her table with a falcon's eye, watching every boiled potato and scrap of meat which usually went into the next day's hash.

Most of her roomers were intimidated by Ma Johnson, which probably accounted for the fact that ninety percent of her renters were bachelors. She took in no female boarders, stoutly asserting that single women had no useful place in society and hinting with clear certitude that those who remained unmarried and not within the sanctity of the parental home were loose women and therefore not welcome under her roof.

She herself was a widow, which fact was commented upon and universally agreed by her roomers, in private of course, that her late husband had taken the easy way out.

Ma Johnson (few of her roomers knew her by any other name) had had two sons and a daughter by the marriage. One son, the oldest, had taken off at the age of fourteen, looking for other things in life besides mother, apple pie and a sometimes leaky roof over his head. The other, a thin, nervous boy with shifty eyes, was the darling of her life. He never complained, he was a good boy, helping her with whatever she wanted. He stole her loose change at every opportunity, but she was blinded by her affection for him and blamed the petty thefts on her only daughter, a fat, sullen-faced girl named Joyce.

Ma Johnson tried to marry her off on every roomer she had with no success. It was one of the reasons the sheriff fled to Cassidy's in the evening and later ought solace in Trimble's *Riviera*.

This evening Cal waited until he heard her scolding her daughter within the confines of her kitchen, then he sneaked down from his room and scurried out, breathing a sigh of relief.

He was totally occupied with his own problems, but he was beginning to think he had things under control. He had the only road leading into and out of town heavily guarded. Sam Bainter had insisted on it and Polly's father, the bank president, had made arrangements with the county to stand part of the additional expense incurred by this.

"What in tarnation's the use of having a local bank if a man can't put his money in it?" John Hansen had bowed to the logic of this. He had a special burglar-proof safe installed, but in the meantime had made secret arrangements with the bigger National Bank in Phoenix to take the cash off his hands. That was why the state bank examiner was coming in some time tomorrow to make his audit.

Cal passed by the bank and checked the guard, finding him dozing, an empty bottle of Tigro by his side. He shook the man awake and was nearly shot as a reward as the startled man jerked his rifle up and fired before he knew what was happening.

"Jesus Christ!" Cal exploded.

The guard apologized. He was feeling poorly (amazing how many of Apache Wells' citizens were feeling poorly these days) and he had had a friend bring him a small bottle of the Professor's pep-up tonic—

"Pep-up, eh?" the sheriff said wrathfully. "Then why are yuh sleeping—?"

The guard promised to stay awake.

THE COFFIN FILLERS

Cal sighed. He looked longingly toward Cassidy's lunchroom, but decided against eating at this time . . . he wasn't really hungry. But he noticed that the horses and burro belonging to Windy and Long Jim were gone. He had a brief moment of relief before he felt the return of anxiety.

Whitey had called them old saddle bums, but they had looked capable enough to him . . . and they hadn't appeared to be the kind who would leave town without their hardware.

"Probably broke in an' took them," he growled. "That's against the law, breaking an' entry. . . ." But he knew he would rather have this than their remaining in Apache Wells. They were a bother, asking about Hardpan Jeffries. With Bighead Nevens and his band of cutthroats in the area, who gave a hang about an old prospector like Jeffries?

He continued on down the road, pausing to eye the crowd around the Professor's wagon. The people who attended were always the same, he noticed. Listening intently, they would back off slightly as the Professor took a deep draft of his magical libation, then deliberately stepped unarmed into the cage with the tiger, who lay like a moth-eaten rolled-up rug in a corner.

"Watch closely now, ladies and gentlemen, as I quell this ferocious beast—this man-eating scourge of darkest Africa—with nothing more than the power of my eyes. . ."

The tiger raised his head slightly and opened an eye. He let out a growl that sounded more like a yawn . . . but the women in the crowd gasped and the more timid pressed back, away from the wagon.

Professor Eccleston crouched before the tiger and the look in his eyes became intense. The tiger dropped his head back and fell asleep. Eccleston straightened, bowed to the scattered applause of the crowd before returning to the small platform in front of the cage.

The sheriff walked away as the Professor began selling his nightly quota of Tigro.

He was worried about Bill. And he dreaded facing Polly tonight and telling her the truth. What in the devil was the truth? Where had Bill gone? The tic under his right eye jumped nervously and he swore with bitter feeling.

He stopped in at *The Riviera* for a drink and Trimble shook his head at his question. Whitey hadn't moved a muscle since they left him on a cot in the back room.

Cal walked down the street to where his office lay dark and uninviting, facing the barren mesa. The stars and a sickle moon painted the backdrop with mystery. The coyote chorus began out on the plain. Here and there a child cried restlessly, voices raised in sudden anger. It was all familiar to Caulkins, sinking out of his consciousness, the sounds and smell of Apache Wells. A breeze felt cool againt his face.

He put his hand on the knob and fumbled for his key. The door opened under his hand. He paused for a moment, searching back in his thoughts. He was sure he had locked it. Then he remembered Whitey had come in here with the guns of the two old strangers and he sighed with resigned acceptance of his deputy's many failings. He went inside and struck a match, lighting the lamp on his desk.

He slumped down in a chair and eyed the paperwork that had piled up on his desk. All his energies, this past week, had been focused on the bank.

Suddenly he became aware of sounds . . . something like a man gargling, then someone thumping against a wall. Cal came alert, his hand sliding down to his gun.

The thumping came from one of the cells. He got up

69

and walked slowly to it, staring through the bars to a shadowy figure on the cot inside.

"Bill!"

His first reaction was relief, then he got peeved. He opened the cell door and went inside. "What in hell yuh doing in here?"

His answer was a vigorous kick in his direction. The sheriff backed off. "Tied up an' gagged." A perverse humor lighted his eyes. "Goddamn it, serves yuh right!"

He bent over his nephew and untied him. Bill sat up and ripped the gag from his mouth, spitting his distate on the floor.

His first words were: "Don't yuh ever come to your office?"

"Wouldn't have come tonight," Caulkins replied calmly, "if I wasn't worried about yuh. Who did it?"

"A pint-sized ol' man who should be home somewhere, in a rocking chair. . . ."

Caulkins grinned. "I see yuh met them."

"Them?"

"He's got a partner . . . a long stringbean about his age. Whitey took their guns. I told them they could have them back when they left town." The sheriff shrugged. "Looks like they've gone."

Bill gingerly fingered the lump on his head.

Caulkins got angry again. "Where've you been? Polly's been hounding me all day. . . ." He wagged his head disapprovingly. "Yuh oughta be ashamed, worrying a fine gal like that. . . ."

"I told yuh where I was going!" Bill snapped.

He walked into the office, found his hat, put it on. Caulkins eyed him wrathfully. "Out chasing after that fool propector? Damn it, I need yuh in town—"

Bill looked mysterious. "Yeah . . . that's what I wanted folks to believe, Uncle Cal."

The sheriff eyed him, feeling suddenly left behind somewhere.

"Believe what?"

"That I was out looking for Hardpan Jeffries," Bill said calmly.

"Well . . . you've been gone two days!" Cal snapped. "Where *have* yuh been?"

"Scouting," Bill said. He lowered his voice, glanced nervously toward the door. "Looking around for Big-head Nevens an' his gang. . . ."

Caulkins' eyes gleamed with sudden admiration. "That was right smart of yuh, Bill. See anything?"

Bill shook his head. "Maybe it's all jest a rumor. Story started in Blind Corners, didn't it?"

Caulkins nodded.

"Could be they're jest disappointed Sam Bainter didn't put his money in their bank, eh?"

Caulkins had never considered this, but he wished Sam Bainter had done just that. He told his nephew this in heartfelt terms.

Bill shrugged.

The sheriff stroked his goatee, suddenly consider-ing the possibilities of this. "Hey," he said as Bill tarted for the door. "Maybe I should pull those guards off duty. They're costing the bank an' the county a heap of money—"

"Hell, don't do that!" Bill said hastily.

"Why not?"

"Well. . . ." Bill's glance picked up the Sharps rifle by the gun cabinet. "Didn't yuh say them two ol' fellers left town?"

Cal was sidetracked by the question. He watched Bill pick up the buffalo gun. "Wouldn't have left this behind, would they, if they were leaving?"

Cal scratched his head, suddenly assailed by a new

71

worry. "They ain't in town," he said, but his tone lacked feeling.

"Yuh sure?"

"I'll check with ol' Moses at the drawbridge. He would have seen them. . . ."

He took the heavy Sharps from Bill, frowned. "Blisters?" He eyed his nephew, wondering. "Looks like yuh been working real hard—"

Bill pulled his hands back. "Yeah. Got them climbing over rocks. Scouting's hard work, Cal. . . ."

He walked behind the desk and picked up his gun. "Yuh keep an eye on them two, Uncle Cal," he warned. "Could be they're in with Bighead Nevens. . . ."

He walked to the door.

Caulkins was still trying to absorb this new turn of events.

"Where're yuh going?"

Bill looked back to him. "Get a good night's sleep."

"Yuh better check in with Polly first," Cal said. "I don't want her after me again tonight. . . ."

Bill grinned, fingered his unshaved jaw.

"Where's Whitey?"

"In Trimble's back room—dead drunk!" Cal said, dis-gust mingling with anger in his voice. "Sent the damn fool out to the mesa to find yuh an' he comes riding back with a crazy story about seeing Hardpan Jeffries' bones—"

The sheriff shook his head. "Yuh go on, make it up with Polly. I'll check on those two ol' codgers who claim to be friends of Jeffries." His eyes narrowed as he reconsidered them. "They ain't as harmless as they seem, Bill . . . not by a long shot!"

72

XIV RUNNING IRON BANK ROBBERS

JEFFRIES' CABIN made a sagging blob of shadow at the base of the mesa as Windy and Long Jim approached it. It was quiet, except for the occasional yipping of a coyote somewhere beyond. The sagging door was open, as they had left it earlier in the day.

They eyed the lonely scene, each man silent for a moment, wrapped in his thoughts. What had started out as a diversion in their wanderings, a reacquaintance with an old friend, had developed into something far more serious.

"Hardpan had his faults," Windy muttered, breaking the silence, "but running out on his obligations wasn't one of them." He turned and eyed his partner, who was slumped in saddle. "Give yuh five to one Jeffries wasn't in Blind Corners yestidday."

Long Jim rubbed the back of his neck. His mouth tasted like it had dry rot and there was a dull ache behind his eyes.

"That's what that long-faced undertaker said—"

"I know what he said," Windy snapped. "But I don't trust a man who wears a shoulder holster and buys his coffins ahead of time."

Long Jim frowned. "Why would that body-snatcher tell us he saw Hardpan in Blind Corners—?"

Windy shrugged. "I don't know. Wanted us out of 'Pache Wells, maybe."

Long Jim dismounted. "He ain't the only one. That winking sheriff wasn't too happy with us neither."

He walked to the cabin and peered inside. It was dark and he couldn't see anything.

"Toss-up," he muttered, turning, "which is better . . . sleeping in here or outside." He shook his head. "Maybe

73

we should have taken our chances in town. I was looking forward to sleeping in a bed for a change."

Windy joined him. "Prob'bly cost us two bucks for a mattress full of fleas." He struck a match and eyed the inside before it flickered out. "Heck, this ain't so bad. Be quiet, anyway."

He struck another match and went inside, moving toward the lantern he had spotted on a shelf. The match went out but Long Jim came up with another. The wick was dry and didn't catch. Windy shook the lantern but got no answering slosh. "Empty," he remarked needlessly.

He struck another match and looked around the cabin. There was a wooden box with a hinged lid in a corner and he opened it. There were some cans inside, and a couple of stubby candles. He lighted one and brought it back to set on the rickety table in the middle of the room.

"Hardpan shore wasn't living high," he remarked.

He walked to the homemade bed against the wall and eyed the straw mattress. A field mouse ran out, squeaking, as he lifted a corner of it.

Windy hauled the old mattress outside and shook it. nothing else emerged. He set it back on the wooden slats.

"Toss yuh for the bed," he said to Long Jim.

Long Jim backed off. "I'll take my chances on the floor."

They went outside and unsaddled the horses and line-picketed them behind the cabin. They brought the stuff from Blinkey's pack inside. They turned the burro loose to forage for himself, knowing out of long experience that Blinky would be back in the morning.

They stared up at the mesa wall. It seemed to loom higher in the night—dark and mysterious, holding its secret of what had happened to Hardpan.

"Whitey saw something up there," Windy muttered.

"We'll look around in the morning," Long Jim said. They went back inside. Long Jim spread his bedroll on the floor. Windy laid his out on the lumpy mattress.

"One thing about Hardpan," Windy remarked, sitting on the edge of the bed, a boot in his hand, "he had a nose for gold."

"An' a temper that got him in a peck of trouble," Long Jim added. He frowned. "Still, he hung around here longer than most places he prospected. Must be he found something. . . ."

Windy's eyes were hard. "That's what I been thinking. An' someone found out about it. . . ."

He settled back on his blanket.

Long Jim moved about restlessly. "Knew we should have stopped off at Cassidy's," he growled. "Never could sleep on an empty stomach."

Windy ignored his partner's complaint. He stared up at the ceiling, his brow furrowing.

"What were yuh doing, prowling around that undertaker's alley?"

Long Jim was silent for a moment, trying to remember. " 'Pears to me I saw something . . . got curious . . . wandered over. Next thing I remember Zack had me on that table of his an' was pouring something down my throat." He made a face. "Then I started chasing them pink cows. . . ."

Windy grunted. "Goat's milk an' *peyote* . . . no wonder. . . ." He blew out the candle, settled himself for sleep. He heard the horses chomping on the feed they had taken along. A coyote barked sharply, somewhere in the night. Then he drifted off.

But Long Jim remained awake, listening to his partner's snores. His stomach growled. He thought of the cans in the supply box. He crawled to it in the dark, felt around, brought one out.

He went outside to open it, using his knife. He was in luck. *Beans!*

He finished the can, crawled back to his blankets. In a few moments he was fast asleep.

The night wore on. The sickle moon slid down out of sight behind a serrated horizon. A coolness spread over the land, dissipating the day's heat.

A figure appeared on the game trail under the mesa wall. It looked down on the cabin below for a moment, then started down the treacherous talus slope. A small rock slide preceded it. The horses behind the cabin raised their heads, listening.

The figure reached level ground and began to limp slightly toward the cabin. Off in the brush Blinky watched him, ears twitching. Suddenly the burro raised his head and brayed loudly.

The figure whirled.

Inside the cabin Long Jim and Windy came awake instantly. They ran for the door in stockinged feet, guns cocked and ready in their hand.

The horses moved restlessly now, behind the cabin . . . one of them whinnied querulously.

Something moved among the shadows beyond.

Windy yelled: "Hey! That yuh, Hardpan?"

The figure began to run back along the base of the slope. Windy fired once, keeping his shot high. The explosion bounced back from the mesa wall. Windy began to run after the prowler. He stumbled, cursed, began to hop around on one foot.

Coming up, Long Jim inquired solicitously: "Stub your toe?"

"Damn cactus!" Windy snapped.

He hobbled back to the cabin and lighted the candle. Long Jim eyed the wicked-looking cholla that clung to Windy's instep.

"Serves yuh right," he grunted, "chasing out there without boots. . . ."

He helped Windy remove the barbs from his foot.

Neither man slept well the rest of the night.

They were up with the first gray fingers of light. Long Jim polished off the two remaining cans, which turned out to be tomatoes. It wasn't the kind of breakfast he liked but he had little choice.

Windy went out into the brush and brought Blinky back to the cabin and tied him up with the saddle horses. The burro thought this a disservice and tried to bite the small man.

He went back and joined Long Jim by the door. Both men stared at the mesa rising sharply against the strengthening daylight.

"Think it was Hardpan last night?"

Windy scratched at his chin whiskers. "Or some varmint out after our cayuses." He frowned. "If it was Hardpan, what's he doing skulking around in the dark like that? Playing peek-a-boo up on that mesa?" He shook his head.

The sky lightened to azure brightness over the mesa. The land and the desert shrubs began to take on color.

"Wish I had my Sharps," Long Jim grumbled. "Ain't nothing more useful to hunt ghosts with. . . ."

They looked for a trail along the base of the mesa and, finding none in the immediate vicinity, decided to make the climb anyway.

It was hard going on the loose shale and steep grade. Long Jim blew noisily as they made the base of the steep cliffs. Windy took off his hat and wiped his brow.

"Must be an easier way up," he muttered. He looked down on the cabin. "If Hardpan was prospecting *on* the mesa, why'd he make his camp down there?"

Long Jim had no answer for him.

They moved along the base of the cliffs on the old game trail. A hawk whirred out of some nesting place above them and both men had their guns out before they realized what had made the sound.

Long Jim looked disgusted. "Ain't nothing up here, Windy—"

He paused as a small rock slide trickled down from above. Both men looked up, but the cliff bulged over them and they could see nothing.

"Something's up there," Windy said. "Watching us. . . ."

They moved more cautiously now, guns held ready, along the game trail. A hundred feet beyond they came upon the cave entrance Whitey had stumbled upon.

Windy stopped, cocked his Colt. Long Jim bumped into him, froze. The sun was still down behind the mesa. The cave was in deep shadow.

Long Jim bent close to Windy's ear. "See anything?" he whispered.

Windy started to move inside the cave. Long Jim tapped him on the shoulder, pointed to something to one side of Windy's boot.

The heel-ground remains of a hand-rolled cigarette!

Windy hunkered down and ran the shreds of tobacco through his fingers. "Not too old," he muttered. "Ain't had a chance to dry out yet. . . ."

Both men peered inside the cave. It was deeper than they had expected, and at the far end they made out a crude wooden ladder resting against the wall. It was little more than a thick pole with cross blocks of wood nailed into it. It led up to a hole in the cave's ceiling.

"Well, I'll be danged!" Windy said. He glanced at his partner. "Reckon that's how that varmint last night got up on the—"

The bullet splatted against the cliff a few feet from

them, ricocheting with an angry whine off the rock wall. Both men whirled.

Sheriff Caulkins and a small posse from Apache Wells were bunched up at the base of the slope just below them.

The sheriff motioned with his rifle. "Come on down, yuh blankety-blank bank robbers!"

Windy turned. The ladder was scraping and bumping along the rock wall, disappearing mysteriously up into the opening in the cave ceiling.

Windy cursed, fired a futile shot at the ladder. A bullet from below splatted closer.

"Be worse for yuh if we have to come up after yuh!" the sheriff yelled.

Windy looked at his partner. Long Jim shrugged. "Told yuh we should have stopped to pick up our rifles—"

They went down to join the posse, sliding and falling part of the way.

Bill Caulkins dismounted and took their guns.

"Salty cuss, ain't yuh, grandpap?" he said to Windy. "Yuh should have left town when yuh had the chance." He grinned. "Reckon there ain't no fool like an ol' one, eh?"

Windy fixed him with a cold stare, then turned to eye Len Stevens among the possemen. The young counter man returned his stare, but he looked uncomfortable.

"Should have jailed yuh right off!" the sheriff said. "Would have saved me a peck of trouble—"

"On what charge?" Long Jim snapped. "We haven't done anything, 'cept look for our friend Hardpan—"

"Breaking an' entering my office," Caulkins cut him off. "Stealing weapons—"

"Them's our guns!" Windy snarled.

"Legally appropriated by the law," the sheriff pointed

out. "Also, I'm jailing yuh on suspicion of being members of Bighead Nevens' bunch of bank robbers!"

"You're loco! We never heard of—"

Bill snapped his cuffs over Windy's wrists. "Yuh can tell your story to the judge, grandpap!" He turned, caught the handcuffs the sheriff tossed to him, and did the same for Long Jim.

Len Stevens and another member of the posse brought their saddled horses, with Blinky trailing, from behind the cabin.

Bill emerged from inside the cabin with the burro's pack load. He was holding a pair of straight irons in his hand.

"Innocent travelers, eh?" He grinned. "What else yuh mavericks do 'sides brand blotting other folks' cows an' robbing banks?"

Windy just shook his head, for once at a loss for words.

Escorted by the posse, they rode back to town.

XV DANGEROUS CHARACTERS

WHITEY HOLLISTER staggered out of *The Riviera*'s back room and paused by the corner of the bar where Trimble was sweeping up. The big saloon owner paused to watch him.

Whitey clung to the bar and looked around with glazed eyes. "Where is it?"

"Where's what?"

"My head," Whitey mumbled. "It jest rolled off. . . ."

Trimble eyed him with a measure of sympathy. He went around his bar. "What yuh need is the hair of the dog that bit yuh," he said amiably. He took a bottle of whiskey from his back shelf and poured a generous shot for the deputy.

"Go ahead," he encouraged. "It'll straighten out your shakes."

Whitey eyed the liquor in the glass, uttered a choked curse and staggered toward the door. Trimble watched him, shaking his head.

"Nothing worse than a teetotaler," he muttered and finished the drink himself.

Whitey came out of the saloon and the early morning sun stabbed into his eyes. He closed them tight while his stomach heaved and rolled over. Then, laying a course to a nearby horse trough through one slit-open eye, he weaved his way to it, dunking his head and shoulders into the water.

A passerby, stopping to look in wonder, pulled the deputy out before he drowned.

Whitey sputtered his thanks. He sat down on the edge of the plankwalk and held his head between his hands.

The Professor, on his way to Cassidy's for breakfast, stopped by and eyed the deputy. "Hung over?" he asked pleasantly. "What yuh need, my friend, is a bottle of my special tonic, Tigro—"

Whitey's fingers clutched at his gun and the Professor beat a hasty retreat, mumbling something about the ingratitude of men and the special stupidity of deputies.

Whitey was still sitting there when the posse rode into town with their prisoners. The sheriff reined aside and looked down at Whitey.

Cal said, "I see you're still alive."

Whitey hung his head.

"Yuh still planning to turn in your badge?"

Whitey considered this in the full light of day. "Wasn't myself last night," he muttered.

"Yuh ain't yuhself any time," the sheriff growled.

Windy said, "Aw, leave him alone, Sheriff."

Caulkins turned in saddle and scowled at the peppery oldster. "Yuh stay out of this!"

Long Jim chipped in, "Hell, he's the only one who's made any sense around here. He saw something up on that mesa yestidday afternoon—"

"That's enough!" Cal said angrily. "I'm tired of hearing about Jeffries' ghost—"

"Well, we ain't!" Windy snapped. "If yuh had any sense you'd be out there seeing what happened to Hardpan, 'stead of jailing his old friends."

The sheriff's eyes narrowed. "That's jest what you'd want, eh—getting me away from the bank an' goose-chasing after that old prospector who's prob'bly in China by now . . .?"

The sudden leap in distance amazed Windy. "China?"

"Well . . . hell. . . ." Cal turned, took out his irritation on his deputy.

"Oughta put yuh out there in the hot sun, guarding the bank," he snarled. "Only yuh ain't in shape to guard anything."

Whitey stood up. "What about them prisoners?"

Cal frowned. "Think yuh can keep an eye on them?"

Whitey nodded.

"They're slippery," Cal warned. "Don't let either of them slick talk yuh into any fool ideas."

Whitey gripped his gunbutt. "I won't."

Cal glanced at his nephew. "That bank examiner's due in today. Once he gets through—"

He cut himself off, scowling as he remembered Windy and Long Jim were present. He turned to Whitey.

"Come on down to the office." Then, taking pity on his hung over deputy, he added in more kindly tone: "I'll have Len bring yuh a pot of coffee from Cassidy's."

THE COFFIN FILLERS

Ten minutes later Whitey, ensconced in the sheriff's chair behind the battered desk, looked up as Stevens came in bringing the coffee.

Long Jim and Windy were seated on a cot in one of the cells. They came to the cell door, looked out.

"Hey!" Windy called. "We haven't eaten since yestidday. Don't we get breakfast?"

Stevens shrugged, looked at Whitey.

"County law," Long Jim said. "Prisoners are entitled to be fed while waiting trial."

Whitey scratched his head. "Reckon that's so," he mumbled. He nodded to Stevens. "Bring them some food."

Stevens headed for the door.

Windy raised his voice. "If yuh bring us any of those beans that Mex cooks up I'll come out an' strangle yuh!"

Stevens grinned. "Yuh talk pretty big for a couple of spavined ol' bank robbers."

"Ain't yuh a mite previous with that kind of talk?" Long Jim snarled. "The bank ain't been robbed yet."

"Nothing like taking a little precaution," Stevens replied. He started to leave.

"Hardpan's still up on that mesa," Windy said. "But I reckon yuh know that, don't yuh?"

Len turned, his eyes hard. "Yuh been seeing things, too?"

"Yeah," Windy snapped back. "Like a prowler around the cabin last night. An' a ladder in a cave this morning, disappearing in a hole in the roof. . . ."

Len shook his head. "Beats hell what folks have been seeing around Jeffries' cabin—"

"We'll beat more'n hell outa somebody when we find out what's going on up there!" Windy snarled. He watched Stevens leave, then he went back to the cot, angry and bitter.

Long Jim walked to the barred window and looked outside.

Windy eyed him. "What yuh thinking, Jim?"

"Food," the long-shanked man said. "What else?"

XVI   GET OUT—AND STAY OUT!

POLLY HANSEN looked up from behind her teller's window as Bill Caulkins came into the bank. There was little business being transacted (in fact there was none) and her eyes sharpened as Bill approached her.

"Yuh oughta be ashamed of yuhself," she greeted him. "Yuh and your uncle. . . ."

Bill was taken back.

"What about?"

"Jailing those strangers. Two harmless ol' people. Is that the way to treat your elders? How will it look in the county paper—Apache Wells unfair to the aged?"

"Whoa!" Bill said. "Maybe they're old, but they're not harmless." He took off his hat and touched the diminishing lump on his head. "One of them banged me on the head last night."

"Yuh probably deserved it," Polly snapped back. "Picking on an ol' man like that." She turned away from him and Bill looked puzzled.

"Gee, Polly . . . what's happened? Uncle Cal said yuh wanted to see me. But last night when I called, your pa threw me out. Said yuh didn't want to see me, and how he was glad yuh had come to your senses."

Polly said stiffly, "Where were yuh the last two days?"

Bill hesitated.

"All right, yuh don't have to tell me. I know all about your carousing in Blind Corners—"

84

Bill cut in angrily: "Damn it, I wasn't carousing any-where—"

A harsh voice interrupted him. "Young man!" He turned as John Hansen approached from his office. Hansen was a tall, powerfully built man with mutton chop gray-ing whiskers, a cold eye.

"Did I hear yuh curse my daughter?"

Bill stuttered, "No-o-o, s-s-sir. . . ."

Hansen turned his attention to Polly. "I thought yuh didn't want to see him?"

Polly's cheeks reddened. She was a stubborn girl and her father couldn't intimidate her.

"I've changed my mind."

Bill stared hopefully. "Polly—yuh mean—?"

"I'll see yuh tonight," Polly said. "After the bank ex-aminer has left."

Hansen's voice was stern. "Polly—yuh know how I feel about this young man—"

Polly interrupted. "We're getting married next week. I've got a right to see the man who's going to be my husband!"

The banker threw up his hands. He turned to Bill. "I'll fire Riles," he said, "an' put yuh on in his place. Least I can do for my daughter."

Riles, the sallow-faced bank teller at the next win-dow blanched.

Bill said angrily, "Damn it, Mr. Hansen, I don't want to work in the bank! I've got a job—"

Hansen fixed him with a cold stare. "Yuh call lazing around on the county payroll a job? I call it useless charity." He turned to his daughter. "If yuh marry him against my wishes you'll have to make your own bed an' sleep in it!"

"I've been doing that since Mother died," Polly re-plied sweetly.

Hansen tried to find words to answer her, managed a growl, and walked back into his office, slamming the door.

Bill said, "I don't need his job, Polly."

Polly smiled. "That's all right, Bill. I'll marry yuh even if you're poor. But a little money coming in helps."

"I ain't gonna be a deppity, either," Bill said stubbornly. "Heck, if it wasn't for this bank robbery scare there wouldn't be enough work for Uncle Cal, let alone Whitey an' me."

He put his hat on, a determined look in his eyes.

Polly's eyes shone with admiration. "What are yuh planning to do, Bill—start a business of your own?" She glanced toward her father's office. "Father says there's a crying need for a good freight outfit in town."

Bill looked mysterious. "We'll see," he said. He looked toward the next teller's cage, but Riles was bending down, moving something around. Bill reached over and gave Polly a quick kiss.

He walked out of the bank, whistling.

Whitey let Stevens in with a breakfast tray for his prisoners. The coffee had revived him somewhat, but his stomach still felt queasy.

Windy, watching from inside his cell, barked: "Where were yuh yestidday afternoon? Prowling around on that mesa?"

Stevens gave him a look.

Long Jim said, "Aw, leave the boy alone."

Stevens left the tray on the desk. "Be seeing yuh," he said cheerfully. He went out.

Whitey brought the tray to the cell door. He set it down on the floor, drew his gun. Unlocking the door, he pulled it open, slid the tray inside with his toe.

Long Jim picked it up.

Windy asked sarcastically, "When do we go 'fore the judge?"

"Ain't no judge in town," Whitey said.

Long Jim was sitting on the cot, the tray on his lap. Windy said, "When's the trial?"

"When the judge gets here. Lessee, around about the middle of October. . . ."

"That's two months from now!" Windy exploded. "Yuh can't keep us locked up until then!"

Whitey locked the cell door.

Windy turned to his partner. "It's all your fault!" he snarled. "Was your idea to visit a spell with Hardpan. . . ."

Long Jim let this go over his head. "Eggs a mite hot, but the potatoes are fine," he said.

Windy stared. "Hot eggs?"

"Peppered up some," Long Jim admitted. He motioned to his partner. "There's a plate for yuh. . . ."

"I jest lost my appetite," Windy said. He shook his head. "Can't that Mex cook put out anything without sprinkling his damned enchilada sauce over it?"

Someone hammered on the outside door. Whitey sidled over to it, hand on his gun. He looked out, frowned, opened it.

Bill Caulkins came in. "Just wanted to see if yuh was awake," he said to Whitey.

"I'm awake," Whitey said. He glanced toward the cell. "An' I'm keeping an eye on them two dangerous characters, like the sheriff said—"

Bill nodded. "Let them out."

Whitey frowned. "Yuh mean . . . let them—"

"I talked to Uncle Cal," Bill cut in. "County can't afford to feed them until the circuit judge shows up."

Whitey hesitated.

Bill took the cell keys from the desk and crossed

to the cell holding Windy and Long Jim. He unlocked the door, stepped back.

"Come on," he said.

Long Jim looked up from the tray; he was going through Windy's breakfast.

"I ain't finished eating—"

Windy took the tray from him and set it aside. "Don't ask questions." He walked into the office, nodded at Bill. "Glad to see the sheriff got some sense for a change."

He started for his rifle by the gun cabinet. Bill headed him off. "I'll take care of your guns." He motioned toward the window. "I have your horses an' that stubborn jackass of yours outside. Give me your word yuh won't start any more trouble an' I'll see yuh out of town."

Long Jim looked at his partner. Windy nodded. "No trouble."

They went outside.

Blinky brayed a welcome as Long Jim and Windy mounted. Whitey watched from the doorway. He looked worried.

"Yuh shore the sheriff said it was all right?"

"Would I lie to yuh?" Bill asked.

Whitey scratched his head. He watched them ride out of town.

Bill escorted the two oldsters as far as the drawbridge. Old Moses unwound himself from his seat in the shade and ambled over to them.

"Let them across," Bill said.

The old man led his team around the turnstile and the bridge creaked and groaned coming down. It settled with a small thud.

Bill handed them their rifles and Colts. "You'll find the shells for them in your saddle bags," he said. His voice was not unfriendly.

"If I ever see Jeffries again, I'll tell him yuh stopped by."

Windy nodded, his eyes guarded.

"Yeah—tell him."

Bill turned to Moses. "If they show up again, don't let them cross. If they get sassy, shoot them. The county'll reimburse yuh."

He waited until Long Jim and Windy crossed over. Moses raised the drawbridge.

Bill waved.

Long Jim and Windy did not wave back.

XVII   THE BANK EXAMINER

WINDY AND Long Jim rode slowly along the road away from the drawbridge. Neither man spoke.

It was noon when they reached a junction in the road. An old wood sign, shot full of holes, pointed northwest. It was unreadable, but they guessed it pointed toward Blind Corners.

Windy studied the sign. Long Jim spat over his horse's ear. Behind them Blinky tugged at his rope and brayed loudly; he was hungry.

Neither man paid any attention to him.

"Hardpan could be in Blind Corners," Long Jim opined.

"He could be in hell, too," Windy said. He was silent a moment, considering. Long Jim looked back toward Apache Wells. The town was hidden in the distance, but the mesa stood out sharply against the horizon.

"There's too many people wanted us out of that town," Windy growled. "That young deppity . . . the sheriff . . . an' a gun-toting, shifty-eyed undertaker. Yuh get slugged because you're nosing around the funeral parlors. We get jailed 'cause we go nosing around Jeffries' cabin." He scratched his head. "An' that Perfessor is still in town, with his tiger an' his tonic. . . ."

Long Jim nodded. "Think there's a connection?"

Windy shrugged. "Might be. But I don't care about their bank . . . I'm caring about what happened to Hardpan." His eyes hardened. "Everybody in town claims he's gone, but everybody talks about his ghost. But a man's ghost don't go prowling around unless he's dead first. . . ."

Long Jim bowed to the logic of this.

"That means somebody killed Hardpan. Probably struck it rich up there, an' the gent who killed him is trying to scare people away. . . ."

"Makes sense."

Long Jim dismounted. He checked his Sharps buffalo gun, reached inside his saddle bag and took out his Colt. He reloaded, slipped it into his holster.

"How we gonna get by Moses at the bridge?"

Windy considered. "There's more'n one way to skin a cat."

Long Jim snorted. "We ain't skinning cats. All we want is to get back into that town without being stopped."

"Same thing," Windy said calmly. He took a bite out of his chewing tobacco. "Maybe we'll have to use that jackass of yours—"

He paused, listening. He grinned. "An' then again, maybe we won't have to do anything."

They pulled off the road, out of sight among the rocks.

The man driving a buggy down the road to Apache Wells resented being sent to this godforsaken desert town as much as he resented the dust and the heat. He was Leroy Madsen, a thin, youngish clerical looking man in high celluloid collar and bowler hat, and he was the bank examiner John Hansen was expecting.

THE COFFIN FILLERS

He'd been stopped twice on the way to Apache Wells by villainous looking men who claimed to be guarding the town from an imminent invasion of outlaws. As far as Leroy Madsen was concerned, the outlaws could have Apache Wells.

He knew he was late and this did not help his temper and he swore that if he was stopped once more, by God—

The two men who stepped out on the road in front of him were an odd and unprepossessing pair. One was long and thin and gaunt, the other short and wiry— and both were old enough, he thought angrily, to know better.

But the rifles they held pointed somewhat carelessly in his direction spoke louder than their voices.

"Yuh the bank examiner the sheriff is expecting?" the smaller man asked.

Leroy nodded, anger darkening his face. He needed a bath, a drink . . . he needed a lot of things, but not another delay.

"I've shown my credentials to guards all along the way," he said coldly. "If yuh don't believe me—"

Long Jim cut in, grinning: "Hell, we believe yuh, mister." He glanced at Windy. "We was sent out here to be your escort."

"Escort?"

Windy nodded, spitting a stream of tobacco juice at an anthill. "Sheriff's expecting trouble. Yuh heard of the outlaw, Bighead Nevens—?"

"Too many times!" Leroy snapped. "Sounds like the kind of story folks tell their children to scare them off to bed."

Windy shot a look at his partner. The bank examiner had a sense of humor.

"Bighead's a bogey-man all right," Long Jim said. "An'

he happens to be lying low somewhere in these hills, waiting for a chance to slip into Apache Wells—"

"What for?" Leroy snarled.

"Yuh oughta know," Windy growled. "Ain't yuh driving in to audit the bank's books? Fifty thousand dollars is a heap of money for most folks."

Leroy nodded. "I just hope he waits until I'm gone before he robs the bank."

Windy looked at Long Jim. "Nice feller," he commented dryly.

Leroy said, "Look, I'm already late. If yuh two want to keep on talking—"

"We're riding into town with yuh," Long Jim said.

Leroy frowned. "Don't yuh own a horse?"

"One a piece," Windy answered. "But I ain't rid in a buggy since I was a boy. Kinda brings me back to my childhood—"

"Back to your dotage, yuh mean!" Leroy sneered. He gulped as Windy's rifle muzzle came up. "Hey, wait a minute, old-timer. I didn't mean anything—"

"You'd do better keeping your mouth shut!" Windy said coldly. "An' listen!"

Leroy nodded, his defiance melting away.

"Down the road a piece you'll come to a bridge. Ain't the kind of bridge yuh generally see around these parts." He paused to shift his chaw of tobacco to his other cheek. "Ol' Moses will ask yuh who yuh are. You'll tell him without no sass. An' when he lowers that drawbridge, be prepared to pay him two bits. Yuh get all that?"

Leroy licked his lips. "Drawbridge?"

"That's what I said." He turned to Jim. "Give us a five minute start. . . ."

Long Jim disappeared among the rocks.

Windy climbed into the buggy behind Leroy. "I ain't

had to shoot a man in the back in a long time," he said amiably. "Don't make me nervous."

Leroy kept his neck stiff, his eyes on the road straight ahead.

"How come?" he asked in a cracked voice. "If you're working for the sheriff, yuh and your friend there don't just ride into town with me?"

Windy cogitated. "Ol' Moses," he said finally. "He's got peculiar ideas about people coming an' going cross his bridge." He put the muzzle of his rifle lightly against the bank examiner's back.

"Let's get rolling."

XVIII   "HE MISSING AGAIN?"

MOSES DOZED in the shifting shade of his lean-to, his stained corncob drooping from a corner of his mouth. He was dreaming of better and younger days and occasionally his wrinkled, blue-veined hands twitched as they clasped the old shotgun across his lap.

He heard the buggy approach through his dreaming. He came awake at once, faded blue eyes snapping expectantly. He shifted his shotgun to target the road across the deep ravine.

The buggy rolled into sight, stopping a few feet from the edge of the road where it dropped steeply into the gully below. The man in town clothes looked down into the "moat," then settled back and stared at the cantilever bridge drawn up on the other side.

Leroy shook his head in self-pity; he wished he had never gone to school and studied reading and arithmetic—

"Yuh wants to cross over?" Moses asked.

"No," Leroy replied. His voice couldn't hold back a

thin, bitter sarcasm. "I drove all the way down here jest for the ride."

"Full of sass, ain't yuh?" Moses said. He spat into the ravine, walked back to his lean-to, sat down.

"Hey!" Leroy called, feeling the prod of Windy's rifle against his spine. "I'm sorry, pop. Guess it's the heat. . . ."

Moses didn't move.

"They're waiting for me at the bank," Leroy pleaded. "Come on, let me cross." Desperation welled up in his eyes as the muzzle prodded harder. "Look, mister . . . I'll pay yuh double what yuh charge. . . ."

Moses then moved. He walked to the drooping-headed team standing by the windlass, grabbed the head stall of the nearest animal and started them on their unending, circular path.

The bridge came down, groaning and complaining, settling with a dust-raising thud.

Leroy drove across. Moses waited just ahead of him, his shotgun held ready across his left arm.

"That'll be four bits, mister."

Leroy hesitated, then reached in his pocket. Behind him Windy slid over the back of the buggy and came quickly around, his rifle pointed at Moses.

The bridge-tender stiffened. Windy walked up to him, took his shotgun. He turned to Leroy.

"Pay him."

Leroy flipped a half dollar to Moses, who caught it expertly, tested it between stubby teeth, pocketed it.

"Get down," Windy told the bank examiner. He pointed to the lean-to. "Might as well wait in the shade . . . both of yuh."

A few minutes later Long Jim showed up, riding his horse and leading Windy's and Blinky. He crossed over the ravine, the shod hooves of the animals thudding hollowly on the heavy planks.

Windy motioned for Leroy and Moses to join him. " 'Pears to be some shade over there," he said, pointing as they came up. "Over by that Joshua tree. . . ."

Leroy stared. "But that's on the other side," he complained.

Windy nodded. "Right yuh are." He motioned with his rifle. "Move!"

Moses and the bank examiner walked right across the bridge. Long Jim went to the turnstile and raised the bridge, cutting off all chance of the two men on the other side crossing back.

Leroy paused. Moses kept walking, shuffling resignedly toward the Joshua tree.

"Yuh can't do this!" Leroy yelled. His voice was shrill. "They're waiting for me at the bank!"

"We'll tell them," Windy reassured.

They tied the buggy animal in the shade of the lean-to, mounted their own cayuses and rode off.

John Hansen glanced at his pocket watch for the tenth time since morning with growing irritation. He was in a bad mood when Sheriff Caulkins stepped inside the bank and asked him a silly question:

"Where's that bank examiner?"

John Hansen ran him out of the bank.

The sheriff retreated up the street, mumbling to himself. It was late in the afternoon, almost the bank's regular closing time, and he was peeved. Things had started to go wrong all day. First, his nephew, Bill had turned the prisoners loose without his say-so. True, Bill had made it sound plausible later, allowing as how the county commissioners would frown on the cost of feeding them, especially one with the appetite of Long Jim, for almost two months.

Bill had personally escorted them across the bridge, assuring Caulkins they wouldn't be back.

Then he had disappeared.

The sheriff stopped in at Cassidy's and eyed the young counter man with bitter regard.

"Where's Bill?"

Len Stevens assumed an innocent expression. "Your nephew?" He shrugged. "Guarding the bank, ain't he?"

"Ain't he, hell!" Caulkins snapped.

"Maybe he's with Polly."

"I was jest in the bank—he wasn't there."

Len sighed. "I don't keep track of your nephew."

"Yuh two have been thick as thieves," Cal started to say, then he stopped, shook his head. "Aw . . . hell . . ." and stamped out of the lunchroom.

Cassidy looked at Stevens. "I wouldn't have his job for the world." He glanced at his only customer, an old man having a bowl of chili. "All I can do is go broke. . . ."

Sheriff Caulkins started up the street for his office. He walked angrily, kicking at stones on the way, the tic twitching madly under his right eye.

A voice called out to him.

He stopped, eyed the horse-faced man standing in the doorway of the *Paradise Funeral Parlors*.

Zack motioned to him. Caulkins scowled.

"Whaddo yuh want, Zack?" he growled, walking toward him.

The undertaker put a cautioning finger to his lips. "Want a word with yuh," he whispered. He glanced toward the black-whiskered guard dozing on the box across from the bank.

"I'm busy," the sheriff snapped.

"Bighead Nevens," Zack whispered. It was a magic word. Caulkins stiffened, his eyes taking on a sharp gleam.

"Where?"

The undertaker stepped inside. The sheriff followed him into the reception room. He looked around. There was a smell of burning incense in the air, but it did not entirely overshadow the odor of a strong cigar.

Cal put his hand on his gunbutt. "If you're playing tricks, Zack—?"

"In there," Zack said quickly. He pointed toward the embalming room. "There's someone who knows exactly where Bighead Nevens an' his men are hiding out."

Caulkins drew his Colt.

"Do I get the reward?" Zack whispered.

"What reward?"

The undertaker looked affronted. "Why, the one they're giving for the capture of Nevens. . . ."

Caulkins pushed him away. He walked on tiptoes across the room, stuck his head through the heavy drapes—

A gunbutt came down across his skull. Someone quickly pulled his limp body out of sight into the embalming room.

Zack smiled coldly. He walked to the door, looked out. There was no one on the street except the sheriff's guard on his box. Zack called to him.

The black-whiskered man got up and sauntered over to the undertaker. After a moment they went inside. . . .

XIX AIN'T NOBODY GUARDING THE BANK

LONG SHADOWS stole across Apache Wells. In the distance Copperhead Mesa glowed red in the rays of the dying sun.

Whitey stirred as he heard someone knock on the office door. He had been dozing, glad to be left alone.

His hangover had receded, but he felt wrung out, depressed. He crossed to the door.

"That yuh again, Bill?" His voice conveyed his irritation; he was not in the mood for company.

The door opened and a gun jammed against his stomach before his hand gripped the latch. He gasped, jerked back. Windy took his gun away from him as Long Jim closed the door behind them and glanced around the office.

"Helluva jail." He grinned. "Always empty."

Windy tossed Whitey's gun into a corner. "Where's the deppity who ran us out of town?"

"Bill?"

Windy nodded.

"Around somewhere." Anger crept back into Whitey's voice. "What yuh two doing back in town?"

"Same as when we first got here," Windy snapped. "Looking for our friend Hardpan."

Whitey gulped. "He's dead."

"Then we want the man who killed him. We figure that might be Bill."

Whitey stared. "Bill wouldn't do that. He was a friend of Hardpan's."

"What about that smart-alecky counter man of Cassidy's . . . Stevens?"

Whitey shook his head. "Stevens, too. He an' Bill staked the old buzzard. Why would they want to kill him?"

"That's what we intend to ask them," Windy said. He motioned with his gun toward a cell.

Whitey balked. "Cal wants me to spell the guard watching the bank. He'll fire me shore if I don't show up—"

"We'll make it up to him," Windy reassured him.

Whitey walked reluctantly into the cell. Windy locked the door.

"Yuh rode out to the mesa to find Bill yestidday afternoon," Windy said. "Yuh didn't find him. But yuh saw Hardpan's ghost. That right?"

Whitey's eyes were sullen.

"Look—I believe yuh," Windy said. "In a cave under the cliffs . . . ?"

Whitey nodded.

"Yuh see a ladder in the cave . . . ?"

Whitey frowned. "No. I saw that skull an' bones. . . . I didn't wait around to see anything else. . . ."

He came to the cell door, gripped the bars. "Yuh believe me. . . . about seeing Hardpan's ghost?"

Windy nodded. Whitey looked relieved.

"We're gonna make a deal with yuh," Windy said. "Yuh stay quiet in there until we find Bill an' we promise to clear yuh with the sheriff. If yuh start hollering an' raising a rumpus we'll come back an blow your head off."

Whitey felt too miserable to protest. "I'll be quiet," he said. He walked back to the cot and lay down.

Len Stevens stepped outside the lunchroom for a smoke. It was a warm, still night. He looked up the street as he lighted up. The bank was closed. Looked like John Hansen had given up on the bank examiner and gone home.

This end of town appeared deserted. But lights were burning in *The Silver Queen* and *The Riviera,* and further up the street, nearer the bank, Zachary Stack's funeral parlors appeared closed for the night.

Penn Trimble came out of his saloon, looked up and down the street. He seemed disconsolate. He spotted Len, waved a halfhearted greeting, and went back inside.

Stevens finished his cigarette, ground it out under his heel. He decided he'd look in on the Professor's last night in town. He knew Cassidy would be looking for him, but he didn't care. After tonight he wouldn't need the job, anyway. . . .

He felt the gun muzzle prod his spine before he heard Windy's voice: "Easy, boy. Step back quietly."

Len did as he was told. He felt a hand on his shoulder, guiding him into the narrow alley alongside Cassidy's. A small kitchen window threw some light into the alley. Through it they could hear the cook's voice rising in singsong discord above the clattering of pans.

Stevens turned to face Windy and Long Jim. He sighed. "What've yuh two doing back in town?"

"We'll ask the questions, sonny," Windy said. "We'll start with your friend Bill. Where is he?"

"I don't know."

"Where's the sheriff?"

"Prowling around somewhere, like he always does." Len eyed them. "Guarding the bank, most likely."

"Ain't nobody guarding the bank," Long Jim said.

Stevens frowned. "It ain't like Cal to leave it unguarded."

"Where's everybody?"

"In Baker's lot, I imagine," Stevens replied. "I hear the Perfessor's giving his tonic away tonight."

Windy scratched at his chin whiskers. "Giving it away, eh?" He looked at his partner and Long Jim nodded. "Same thing happened in Tucson. . . ."

Len said, "What happened in Tucson?"

Windy hooked his front sight into Stevens' stomach. "The bank's none of our business, feller," he growled. "Hardpan is. An' we figure your friend Bill knows what happened to him. You're gonna help us find him."

Len hung back. "I can't leave here. Cassidy needs me."

Windy sneered. "What for? Hold his hand?"

Len shook his head. "Look, you're making a mistake. Bill is a friend of Jeffries . . . he wouldn't hurt him."

"Then where is Hardpan?"

Len's mouth closed tight.

Long Jim's eyes hardened. "All right, sonny. Come along. We'll find Bill if we have to turn this town inside out!"

XX TIGER ON THE LOOSE

CASSIDY CAME out of his back room chewing on a cigar and stared morosely along the row of empty stools in front of the counter. Not that he was expecting any business tonight. He was resigned to that fact as long as the Professor remained in town. But he did expect the men he hired to be on the job, just in case.

He stuck his head inside the kitchen opening and inquired of the cook the whereabouts of Len Stevens; he received, in reply, a barrage of words, mostly unprintable, and retreated, mentally vowing he'd fire his cook the first chance he got.

Cassidy wandered outside. It was quiet at this end of town. Only *The Riviera* and *Gertie Lou's Silver Queen* showed lights. He knew they weren't doing any business, either.

Stevens was nowhere in sight.

Damn that kid, he thought, *probably sneaked across the street for a drink. . . .*

He started for Trimble's saloon, but stopped in the middle of the street as he heard a door open further up. A dark figure with huge shoulders appeared briefly in the doorway of the *Paradise Funeral Parlors,* then ducked quickly back inside. A moment later Zack appeared. He waved casually to Cassidy and Cassidy waved back.

"Quiet tonight, eh?" Zack said.

Cassidy nodded. "Too damn quiet!"

He headed angrily for *The Riviera*.

It was quiet inside *The Silver Queen,* too. Too quiet. Gertie Lou took a nip from her private bottle and wandered to the door of her office and looked out into the empty barroom.

She called to her bartender.

No one answered.

She called again, her voice booming across that empty room.

The front door opened and Cassidy came inside. He stopped by the bar and looked toward Gertie.

"Yuh see Stevens in here a few minutes ago?"

Gertie padded toward him in her stockinged feet. "Ain't seen nobody all day," she grumbled. She went behind the bar and peered under the counter, looking for her bartender.

"Yuh see Jerry?"

Cassidy shook his head. "He gone, too?"

Gertie eyed the lunchroom owner. "Gone where?"

"Baker's lot," Cassidy said. "Like everybody else."

Gertie straightened to her full, awesome height. "Yuh mean he's out there, swilling that poison the Perfessor calls his tonic—?"

Cassidy nodded, scowling. "I hear the Perfessor's got a special on tonight—"

This was too much for Gertie Lou.

She brushed Cassidy aside, ran back to her office, pausing just long enough to put on her boots, jam a flower-decked straw hat on her head, and check the derringer she wore in a holster strapped to her thigh under her dress.

She marched out, heading for Baker's lot with blood in her eye!

THE COFFIN FILLERS

Smoke from a half dozen torches lighting Baker's lot drifted across Custer Avenue. The Professor's last night in Apache Wells was a gala affair. Practically all of the town's inhabitants were crowded around his wagon and the tiger cage behind it.

The Professor was in fine form. In gratitude for the fine reception he had received here, this night, his last night here . . . he was including, absolutely free, with every bottle of Tigro sold, another bottle of his marvelous tonic. . . .

Long Jim, Windy and Len Stevens watched from the back of the crowd. Neither Windy nor Long Jim were interested in the Professor's spiel. . . .

Windy shoved his gun against Len's back. "We've been all over town," he said coldly. "Now we quit playing games. Yuh tell us where Bill has gone, or I put a hole through the back of your shirt right now!"

Stevens licked his lips. The man was serious.

"Look, mister . . . Hardpan isn't dead. Bill just wanted yuh out of town for a while. . . ."

"Why?"

Len hesitated. "Bill's gone back up the mesa—"

A massive arm shoved him rudely aside as Gertie Lou hit the edge of the crowd. She plowed toward the Professor's wagon like a battleship, scattering spectators before her, stopping only when she was within a foot or two of the tiger cage.

The door was held closed by a simple hasp with a peg pushed through it. The Professor had never felt the need of a padlock.

Eccleston turned on his platform to survey the angry woman.

"Madam," he admonished sharply as Gertie eyed the hasp, "I must advise yuh to keep away from Leopold. He has clawed more than one curious spectator—"

103

The tiger was pacing within the confines of his small cage. He had not yet been fed and he was hungry.

Gertie Lou sneered. "He has, has he?" With a quick motion she reached up and pulled the peg free. Swinging the cage door open she stepped back, her voice blaring belligerently: "Get out of there, yuh mangy tomcat!"

A curious fascination, compounded of fear and shock, held that crowd immobile. The tiger crouched. He was an old cat who had been in captivity so long he had forgotten what freedom was. In the stillness of that moment his long tail thumped audibly on the wooden floor. Then he snarled, a silent wrinkling of lips, and paced to the door. . . .

The crowd disrupted into fleeing units, as if expelled by centrifugal force toward Custer Avenue.

Leopold hesitated in the doorway. Gertie was backing up, clawing under her dress for her derringer.

"Get away from me, yuh moth-eaten parlor rug—"

The tiger jumped down. She fired, and missed. But the sharp crack from the derringer sent the tiger cringing under the wagon.

Someone let go with a shaky .45. The bullet gouged splinters from a rear wheel, sending the frightened cat bounding toward the darkness of a rear alley.

In the pandemonium that followed no one paid any attention to the heavy dynamite charge that blew open the bank's safe, nor noticed the half dozen hard-eyed outlaws who broke out of the bank and ran across the street to the *Paradise Funeral Parlors*. . . .

XXI ONE CORPSE TO A COFFIN

FEAR GRIPPED a tense Apache Wells. Women barricaded their doors and windows while trigger-happy men took potshots at everything that moved.

Windy and Long Jim moved cautiously out of the darkness of an alley and started across the street for Cassidy's. They had lost Stevens in that first mad rush of the crowd ... they were looking for him.

A stentorian voice up the street bellowed: "There he is . . . heading across the street . . ." and a flurry of shots whistled their way.

Both men cursed as they ducked back into the shadows and ran along the walk to the *Paradise Funeral Parlors*. It was the only refuge handy at the moment. They found the door bolted, and they pounded on it.

The undertaker opened the door. Both men shoved past him, and Zack quickly closed the door and turned. There was a lamp on the organ, turned low. Cigar smoke lingered in the air.

Zack stared at the two oldsters. "Thought you'd left town . . . ?"

Windy brushed that aside.

The undertaker motioned toward the door. "What's going on out there?"

"The Perfessor's tiger's on the loose!" Windy growled. "Whole town's gone crazy. They're shooting at every shadow that moves, an' even those that don't!"

Stack looked nervous. "Well, yuh can't stay in here. Ain't got room for yuh." He grinned weakly. "Less'n you're a corpse."

Long Jim grunted. "We'll wait here until things quiet down outside—"

He paused and Windy frowned as a peculiar drumming came from inside the embalming room.

"What's that?" Windy asked.

Zack ran his tongue across his lips. "I don't hear anything. . . ."

Long Jim pointed toward the back room. "In there." He turned to the stiff-faced undertaker. "Sounds like one of your customers doesn't like the way his box fits. . . ."

Stack backed off a bit. "Yuh must be hearing things. Nothing back there but empty coffins—"

He made a stab for his shoulder gun, and Long Jim jammed the muzzle of his gun with savage force into his stomach. The undertaker gasped. He started to wilt, his stovepipe hat tumbling from his head. Windy slashed him across the head with the side of his Colt and the undertaker collapsed.

There was a moment of silence as the two old reprobates looked at each other. Then the drumming continued.

Windy made a motion with his head toward the back room. Long Jim nodded.

Gun in hand, they walked silently to the heavy black drapes, parted them, looked inside.

The drumming seemed to come from one of the coffins. Windy walked slowly to the musical box while Long Jim hung back, eyeing the others.

The cover was not nailed on. Windy slid it back.

Sheriff Caulkins, trussed and gagged, knees slightly doubled, glared up at him. A gurgle escaped through his gag.

Windy sat down on the edge of the casket, shaking his head in wonder. "I'll be damned," he said peevishly. "Looked all over town for yuh. What yuh doing in this box? Trying it on for size?"

The sheriff's angry gurgling mingled with the faint

rustling and tapping in another coffin. Windy's eyes widened. He looked up as Long Jim joined him. "Damn place is alive with them. . . ."

He cut the sheriff free with a pocket knife and stepped back as Cal sat up and ripped the gag from his mouth.

Caulkins stepped out of the box. He looked frightened. He made a motion toward the door, waving frantically for Windy and Long Jim to follow.

"What's the matter?" Windy growled. "Lose your tongue?"

"Shh!" the sheriff whispered. "We got to get out—"

"What in hell yuh whispering for?" Windy asked loudly. "Hell, we ain't leaving here tonight . . . not with that tiger running loose out there—"

He paused, sensing Long Jim stiffen against him. There was a sudden clattering among the coffins as covers were thrown aside.

Bighead Neven and his five killers stepped out of the caskets and ranged themselves along the wall near the open back window. Drawn guns glinted menacingly in the lamplight.

"Don't know how yuh got wise to us," the big outlaw said bitterly, "but I reckon we'll have to fit yuh two snoopers, along with the sheriff, permanently into a couple of these boxes—"

A volley of pistol and rifle shots, bursting in the street just outside the funeral parlors, interrupted him.

A voice yelled: "There he goes!" and more shots slashed the stillness.

Bighead Nevens frowned. "What the hell's going on—"

There was a quick, heavy padding in the alley under the window. The outlaw leader turned, his Colt cutting up. Two huge paws appeared on the sill, and a moment later a huge, black-striped head appeared in the opening. A pair of cruel, unblinking eyes stared into the room, freezing the men nearest the window.

A shot whanged harshly down the alley and the big cat scrambled over the sill. It hesitated, forepaws on the rim of the sink just below, snarling defiance.

Nevens fired instinctively . . . the slug ripping into the tiger's chest. The cat came off the sink in one long leap for the outlaw's throat. Nevens fired again, then went down with the big cat snarling over him.

The men behind Nevens scattered and broke for the door. Windy and Long Jim met the charge behind blazing guns.

Minutes later Trimble, leading a party of riflemen, cautiously entered the *Paradise Funeral Parlors* and pushed aside the curtains of the inner room.

Gunsmoke was slowly filtering out through the alley window, like a dissipating fog.

The men paused, staring down at the tiger sprawled across Nevens' body. The outlaw chief's throat had been slashed open by savage fangs and blood made a thick, dark pool under him. In various positions around the room were other corpses.

Windy and Long Jim were sitting on a coffin. Windy's left arm hung limp, blood trickling down his fingers. Long Jim was tightening a neckerchief around the upper part of Windy's arm to stop the bleeding.

The sheriff was sitting on another coffin, his head in his hands. There was a lump the size of a goose egg on his head and he was suffering from shock, but otherwise he was unhurt.

Windy looked up at the men crowding the curtained doorway. "Yuh came a little late," he growled. "The *soiree's* over."

Trimble said, "Looks like a massacre." He walked to the tiger and nudged the dead animal with his foot.

Recognition slackened his heavy face. "I'll be damned! It's Bighead Nevens himself!"

Someone poked around the coffins and found the black-whiskered guard the sheriff had left to guard the bank. Someone else came up with a couple of canvas sacks filled with money.

"Holy jumping catfish!" the man exclaimed. "They must have busted the bank an' we didn't even know it!"

The sheriff finally got his tongue working. "Bunch of nitwits!" he snapped. "Whole town's full of nitwits!" He glared at Windy. "Where's Whitey?"

"Taking things easy in your office." He tossed the cell keys to the sheriff.

"How in hell did Nevens an' his bunch get into town without one of the trail guards giving the alarm?" asked Cassidy. The lunchroom owner had just come in and was staring at the bodies.

The sheriff jerked a thumb to the undertaker, who had stumbled in, holding a hand to his head. The man's eyes were glazed . . . he didn't seem to understand what had happened.

"Zachary brought them in. Smuggled the whole crew into town right under our noses . . . in those empty coffins. Reckon he was aiming to get them out the same way—"

Trimble shook his head. "Well," he said judiciously. "They'll be filling them coffins permanently now."

There was a commotion in the doorway and a high-pitched voice said: "Outa the way, folks. I got news!"

Heads turned to view a wizened, leathery-faced man about Windy's size and general shape who limped into the room. A dozen voices merged with Windy's and Long Jim's:

"*Hardpan!*"

Bill Caulkins came in behind the old prospector with

Len Stevens a step behind. Hardpan stared at the scattered corpses.

"Dang it, I knew I'd miss something. Heard the racket as me an' Bill was riding into town—"

"We thought yuh was dead!" accused Windy. "How come you're alive?"

Hardpan chuckled. "Jest a joke Bill, Len an' me cooked up. Ran into pay dirt up on the mesa. Didn't know jest what I had, so we figured if I played dead a while I'd get time to work the vein, find out how rich it was, an' get it all staked out 'fore I came to town to file on it. Hey!" He shook his head as practically every man in the room stampeded out to look for shovels, picks and other paraphenalia needed to stake out a claim.

He turned to Windy and Long Jim, grinning: "Recognized yuh yestidday afternoon when yuh rode up to the shack. That's why I come to town now, to—"

"To celebrate," interrupted Penn Trimble with a smile. The bulky saloon keeper had not gone charging out after the others, knowing there was no need for him to do so. Whatever gold was found on the mesa would come trickling in across his bar.

"Let's retire to my place," he suggested. "The drinks are on the house tonight. . . ."

Long Jim and Windy stayed for the wedding. Hardpan Jeffries was Bill Caulkins' best man. He looked uncomfortable in cutaway coat, silk shirt and top hat. But John Hansen had insisted . . . and few men argued with the town's banker.

Hardpan sneaked away from the reception and joined Windy and Long Jim at *The Riviera* for a drink. "Like ol' times," he said, but he didn't look happy.

Windy shook his head.

"Stick around," Hardpan said. "I'll make yuh partners—"

"Yuh got two partners already," Windy pointed out. "The sheriff's nephew, an' the Stevens kid."

Hardpan sighed. "Yeah, that's right."

He walked to the door with them.

"Come by some time?" His voice sounded wistful.

Long Jim and Windy mounted. Behind them Blinky brayed impatiently.

Long Jim waved. Windy said: "Sure, Hardpan . . . we'll be back . . . someday. . . ."

Jeffries watched them ride out of town. He wandered back into *The Riviera*.

"Best friends a man ever had," he said to Trimble. Then, pushing his glass toward the big man: "Fill it up, Penn. I'm good for it. . . ."

Peter B. Germano was born the oldest of six children in New Bedford, Massachusetts. During the Great Depression, he had to go to work before completing high school. It left him with a powerful drive to continue his formal education later in life, finally earning a Master's degree from Loyola University in Los Angeles in 1970. He sold his first Western story to A.A. Wyn's Ace Publishing magazine group when he was twenty years old. In the same issue of *Sure-Fire Western* (1/39) Germano had two stories, one by Peter Germano and the other by **Barry Cord**. He came to prefer the Barry Cord name for his Western fiction. When the Second World War came, he joined the U.S. Marine Corps. Following the war he would be called back to active duty, again as a combat correspondent, during the Korean conflict. In 1948 Germano began publishing a series of Western novels as Barry Cord, notable for their complex plots while the scenes themselves are simply set, with a minimum of description and quick character sketches employed to establish a wide assortment of very different personalities. The pacing, which often seems swift due to the adept use of a parallel plot structure (narrating a story from several different viewpoints), is combined in these novels with atmospheric descriptions of weather and terrain. *Dry Range* (1955), *The Sagebrush Kid* (1954), *The Iron Trail Killers* (1960), and *Trouble in Peaceful Valley* (1968) are among his best Westerns. "The great southwest . . ." Germano wrote in 1982, "this is the country, and these are the people that gripped my imagination . . . and this is what I have been writing about for forty years. And until I die I shall remain the little New England boy who fell in love with the 'West,' and as a man had the opportunity to see it and live in it."